UNEXPECTED SERENITY

JACQUELIN THOMAS

Chapter 1

CHARLESTON SOUTHERN UNIVERSITY, the only Christian College in the low country, covered three hundred acres. Nicholas Washington drove through the entrance, parked in the designated space for the chair of the English department and got out of his vehicle.

Housed inside the College of Humanities and Social Sciences, his office was long and narrow, with wide, wood plank flooring, covered by a colorful woven rug he purchased while on a trip to Ghana. A big, comfortable couch and two chairs, upholstered in a soft, burgundy-colored fabric were positioned against the wall near the door. Floor to ceiling shelves filled with books of all shapes and sizes, paperback and hardback lined the back wall.

Nicholas sat down at his desk and turned on his computer. It thrilled him to be back in Charleston after a ten-year absence. He'd spent his time away working on a new mystery series while teaching at UCLA in California. Nicholas enjoyed living in Los Angeles but couldn't forget the charm of Charleston, South Carolina, nor ignore the love he felt for Shelia Moore. They initially kept in touch after he left town, but the conversations waned, then completely dissipated five years ago.

A soft knock on the door of his office captured his attention.

"Professor Washington?"

Nicholas glanced up from his monitor to a young woman dressed in jeans and white tee-shirt beneath a navy-blue cardigan. Her locs were thin and neat, reaching down to her waist. "Yes. How can I help you?"

"My mom asked me to introduce myself."

He nodded complacently while quietly observing her. There was nothing familiar about this young woman, but she'd gained his interest. Was her mother someone he knew or was she just a fan of his books?

As if she could read his mind, she said, "My name is Kiya Moore. Sheila is my mother."

His eyebrows rose in surprise. "You're Sheila's *daughter*?"

She gave a slight nod. "I am."

Nicholas stared wordlessly at her, his heart pounding.

"She adopted me and my brother Gray five years ago." Kiya smiled. "I'm a freshman here and I'm really looking forward to your creative writing class. I want to be a writer."

He recovered quickly and found his voice. "Kiya, it's very nice to meet you. Sheila never told me she was thinking of… anyway, how is your mother?"

It almost seemed too good to be true. "I'd planned to drive to the Mt. Pleasant area this weekend to see if your mother still lived in the same house."

"We do," Kiya responded. "My mama's doing great. She still has those moments when the pain is unbearable, but you know her—she's a fighter."

He grinned. "Yes, she is…"

"I can give you her number if you'd like to reach out," Kiya offered. "I have her permission."

"I'd like that," Nicholas responded with a smile. It was a sign, he decided.

Kiya gave him Sheila's phone number.

"Thank you," he said. "It's really nice to meet you, Kiya. I'm looking forward to having you in class. I reviewed your sample, and you truly have a gift, but I want you to stretch yourself more—especially if you want to be a writer."

"I'm excited to get started," she gushed. "Thanks for the advice, Professor Washington."

"Thank you for coming by, Kiya. It's a pleasure to meet you."

Smiling, she said, "I'll see you in class tomorrow morning."

Nicholas gave a slight nod. "Eight a.m."

When Kiya left his office, he exhaled a short sign of contentment as he stared at Sheila's number. Nicholas wanted to call her right this minute, but he had a busy day ahead. However, he had no intentions of letting this day end without talking to her.

It had been too long.

A WARM GLOW flowed through Sheila when she read her daughter's text. *I can imagine Nicholas's surprise when Kiya shared that I was her mother.*

According to her daughter, he seemed eager to reconnect with her.

She gathered her strength, got out of bed and strolled barefoot across the room with the aid of her cane to the bathroom. Because of the instability of her gait, Sheila used an assistive device on a daily basis. Having had to use a walker for the previous three years—she was grateful to only have need of a cane. It was a small reprieve but Sheila considered it a huge blessing.

She showered and was dressed by the time her housekeeper arrived.

"I didn't expect you up this early."

Sheila smiled, her mood buoyant. "Today is a good day, Valerie. I'm not feeling tired and weak. But most of all, I'm not in any pain."

"I'm glad to hear this. We've been praying for your healing every week at intercessory prayer."

"Thank you. I truly appreciate the prayers."

Valerie strode into the kitchen. "What would you like for breakfast, Miss Moore?"

"An omelet. Spinach, tomatoes, mushrooms and bacon," Sheila responded.

"Egg whites and cheddar as usual?"

"Yes please."

"I left my medicine in the bedroom," Sheila announced. "I'll be right back so we can go over the grocery list."

Retrieving the eggs, cheese and other ingredients from the refrigerator, Valerie responded, "Breakfast will be ready shortly."

Sheila cherished her housekeeper. She was good about prepping ingredients ahead of time and was extremely organized. They spent each Monday morning preparing the menu for the week. She would pick up the necessary items and then prep the food. Valerie pretty much ran the household for Sheila—she also drove Sheila to all of her appointments. Although her doctor was okay with it, Sheila made the decision to stop driving six months ago. She felt it was best because multiple sclerosis could be unpredictable.

When she returned, Valerie had a bowl of fruit waiting for Sheila. "Your omelet's coming up in two-seconds."

After her breakfast, Sheila and Valerie composed a menu for the week.

"I'm in the mood for some of your fried chicken."

"Do you want that for dinner tonight?"

Sheila grinned. "Yes please."

They made small talk as they compiled a shopping list. "Oh, we need more eggs," Sheila said.

"Anything else?" Valerie asked.

Sheila reviewed the items. "I think that's it. Oh, Kiya had an opportunity to speak to Nicholas. He's going to call me."

Valerie broke into a smile. "I told you it would work."

"Thank you for the suggestion. When Kiya ended up in his class—I felt it was confirmation."

"This time don't run away," Valerie told her.

"I won't," Sheila responded. "But I'm not going to run into his arms either. Nicholas and I haven't spoken in five years. We've both changed and we need to get to know one another again."

"I agree." Valerie stood up and walked over to the kitchen counter. "I'ma head on to the store before it gets busy. It's double coupon day."

"I need to get on a zoom call with Jake and Margo in about five minutes."

In her office, Sheila sat at her desk waiting to be logged into the meeting. There was a time when seeing Jake Madison would put a huge smile on her face—a time when she thought he meant the world to her. Now she knew better.

Jake was her business partner and nothing more. The feelings she once felt for him were gone. The only man taking up permanent residence in her heart was Nicholas.

The meeting of the partners lasted about ninety minutes. Sheila didn't personally handle any of the projects anymore, instead she was a consultant to the company.

She heard Valerie humming in the kitchen. Sheila smiled, then returned her attention back to the reports Jake sent over.

"Has Professor Washington called you yet?" Kiya asked when she checked in with Sheila shortly after twelve noon.

"No, but I don't really expect to hear from him until sometime later, especially with classes starting tomorrow."

"He seemed pretty excited about reconnecting with you."

She broke into a smile. "That's the second time you mentioned that. Sweetie, Nicholas has always been a sweetheart and a real friend. Let's not read too much into this dinner."

"Mama, you always say that. I feel like you're downplaying how you really feel about him."

Sheila's heart swelled with pride. Her daughter had always been very astute. "I have deep feelings for him, but our time has already passed."

"You still love him."

"I do," Sheila confessed. "I'll always love Nicholas, but as I said... we had our chance years ago."

"It's never too late for love."

"What do you know about love?" Sheila asked with a soft chuckle.

"Just what I've read in novels. Mama, I know for sure that you're beautiful and you have so much love to give—you deserve to find happiness with someone like the professor."

"You're so sweet, Kiya."

"It's the truth."

Sheila smiled. "You know I feel the same way about you. You're my beautiful girl and the man you fall in love with— he's going to really need to be something pretty special." She shifted her position. "Did you get all of your textbooks?"

"I did," Kiya responded. "And I've already finished the required reading for freshmen."

Sheila had so much fun helping her daughter move into her dorm room and decorating. Although she didn't live far from the university, Sheila wanted Kiya fully immersed into being a college student. She missed having her at home though. Her son was a junior in high school but spent most of his time working and playing sports. Keeping Gray busy kept him out of trouble.

Sheila spent the rest of her afternoon swimming back and forth in her pool. The water did wonders for her aching limbs. She eased out of the water and sat down on a lounge chair, fully relaxed. Her eyelids grew heavy, and she fell asleep outside in the shade.

Valerie gently awakened her an hour later. "I made you some lunch, Miss Moore. It's almost time for your medication."

"Thank you," Sheila said with a smile. "I don't know what I'd do without you. You always take such good care of me."

"My sister has multiple sclerosis, so I know what you have to deal with. I'm glad I can be of service to you."

"I appreciate you." Sheila rose to her feet and followed the woman into the house. "Give me about ten minutes to freshen up."

She went upstairs and quickly changed out of the wet swimsuit, took a quick shower, then slipped on a sundress in a vivid sapphire blue. She stuck her feet in a pair of gold flip flops.

Downstairs, Valerie had a Caesar salad with blackened shrimp, garlic bread, and iced tea waiting for her.

"The fried chicken is in a bowl on top of the stove. I made some green beans and mac and cheese to go with it. Would you like me to make some yeast rolls?" Valerie asked.

"No, you don't have to do that," Sheila responded. "We're good, but thanks for asking."

"When will Gray be home?"

"Right after football practice. He's only working week-ends now that school's about to start."

"I can hardly believe that Kiya's in college and Gray is a junior in high school. Those five years flew by in a blink of an eye."

Sheila nodded in agreement. "Way too fast."

Valerie checked her watch. "Well, I guess I need to head on home. You're sure you don't need anything?"

"I'll be fine," Sheila responded. "Thank you. Be safe."

"Hey Miss Val… Mama…" Gray said when he entered the house.

"Hey sweetie." Sheila wrinkled her nose. "Oooooh…you smell like a man… go on up and take a shower. I'll heat up dinner."

Valerie chuckled. "I'll see you tomorrow."

Sheila had dinner on the table when Gray returned.

They sat down to eat.

Gray blessed the food.

"How was practice?" she inquired.

"Same as always. Coach worked us hard."

"The team looks good this year," Sheila stated. She'd attended all of the scrimmages and looked forward to watching her son play.

"Yeah, we got some decent players. Our first game is in two weeks, so we'll see."

After they finished eating, her son cleaned the kitchen.

They watched a movie afterward.

It was almost nine o'clock. Gray began focusing on his phone, so Sheila planted a kiss on his forehead, then navigated to her room. She glanced at her cell phone; something she'd done several times in the past couple of hours. Sheila had hoped to hear from Nicholas by now—maybe Kiya had been wrong about his eagerness to reconnect. Maybe he took her number to be polite.

She was about to prepare for bed when the phone rang.

"Hello…"

"Sheila, it's so good to hear your voice."

The mere sound of his voice gave her joy. "Nicholas, I wasn't sure you were going to call."

"There's no way I'd ever come back here and not contact you. I'd planned to call you earlier, but had a lot going on today."

His voice was still as soft as a caress. "It's good to hear from you."

"How have you been?"

"Nicholas, I'm fine, but I don't want to spend this time talking about my health. Tell me about you. What have you been up to?"

"Teaching and writing," he responded with a chuckle. "That's about it."

"I'm surprised you decided to leave Los Angeles behind. You seemed to really enjoy living out there."

"It's a great place to live but I really love Charleston."

"I feel the same way," Sheila said. "I love everything about this city from the cobblestone streets, the restaurants, beautiful sandy beaches and charming historic district."

"The first thing I did when I came back was go to the Tattooed Moose for a burger."

"That's one of Gray's favorite places to eat. He has to have his with a side of duck-fat fries."

"Yep..."

"I miss eating at Coast Bar and Grill, then going to King Street for live music," Sheila stated.

They continued to reminisce over the many memories they created together.

THE SOUND of Sheila's voice still made Nicholas's heart flutter after all these years.

"I have to admit I was very surprised to hear that you have children," he said.

"I figured you would be," Sheila responded. "To be honest, I shocked myself when I decided to adopt. I'd been thinking about adopting for a while, so I focused on that. We weren't communicating anymore, so I focused on building a family."

"We didn't have to stop talking Sheila."

"Nicholas, you'd met someone, and it seemed like you really cared about her. I couldn't just be your friend... I wanted more from you. I thought it was best that I move on with my life."

"I wouldn't have abandoned you."

"I know that, but I didn't want to complicate your life and I probably would have tried back then."

"As you see, it didn't work out."

"If I said I was sorry to hear that, I'd be lying."

He chuckled. "Same Sheila..."

"I'm definitely not the same woman I used to be, but in all honesty, there are some things that will never change, Nicholas."

"I wouldn't have it any other way."

"You say that now…"

There was a short pause.

Nicholas cleared his throat noisily. "I'm looking forward to having Kiya in my class. I had all the students complete writing samples. When I read hers... Sheila, it blew me away. She wrote about the day she and her brother were informed someone wanted to adopt them. She shared how the three of you went to counseling together to ensure you were fit to be their mom. Kiya said the three of you bonded instantly because each of you in your own way were hurting and broken. But now, you're a perfect fit in all areas that matter. Of course, I didn't know at the time she was talking about you specifically."

"Kiya told me that's what she wanted to submit. When I read the first draft—she had me in tears. My daughter is a truly talented writer. The first time they were able to visit me —she saw your books on my shelf and was so excited. She'd read all of them which surprised me. Kiya was only thirteen at the time."

"If you don't mind my asking what happened to their parents."

"Their mother shot their father—she was tired of the physical abuse. She then killed herself. Thankfully, the children weren't home at the time. Since they had no family, they were placed in a group home. I heard about what happened on the news and contacted social services. I figured I'd be better with older children because of my struggles with multiple sclerosis. Kiya's right. The three of us bonded immediately."

"I know that you're a wonderful mother."

"This almost feels like old times," Sheila murmured. "You've always had such faith in me."

"That won't ever change," Nicholas assured her. "I have to say that I've really missed our chats. I've missed you."

"Same here," she murmured.

"Let's talk about your health."

"Do we have to?" Sheila responded.

"How are you really doing?"

"I still have good days and bad, Nicholas. Things could always be worse, I suppose, so I try not to complain."

"If you're feeling up to it, I'd like to have dinner with you one night this week," Nicholas said.

"I'd love it."

"Which night works best for you?" he asked.

"Tomorrow night is good."

"Great," he exclaimed with pleasure. Nicholas was looking forward to seeing Sheila again.

Chapter 2

SHEILA TURNED up her smile a notch as she hung up the phone.

Pure bliss was the best way to describe what she was currently feeling. She wanted to dance around her bedroom, but wisdom prevailed. She didn't want to end up on the floor.

She'd been honest about missing him and their frequent phone conversations, but the reason why she stopped communicating with him was because it hurt too much—the idea of Nicholas dating. He'd had every right to do so because their relationship had ended. However, the love she felt for him never dissipated.

Sheila navigated to her bathroom and removed her clothes.

She stepped carefully into the tub, closed her eyes and slid down under the bubbles.

After her bath, she dried off, slipped into a pair of silk pajamas and eased into her king-sized bed. She was tired of sleeping alone. Sheila hadn't completely given up the idea of getting married and she'd had a couple of opportunities over the years, but her heart belonged to Nicholas.

"I'm scared," she whispered. "I love him so much, but I just don't want to mess up. I can't take losing him all over again."

She threw the covers over her face and blocked out the world. For now, Sheila wanted to relish her never ending fantasy of the life she could've had with Nicholas—the two of them raising Kiya and Gray, traveling the world and growing old together.

They had been given a second chance. Sheila vowed she wouldn't make the same mistake this time.

———————

"So, what are you wearing for your date tonight?" Kiya asked. She'd come to the house after her last class to help her mother get ready.

"I don't know," Sheila responded. "Hon, it's not a real date… Nicholas and I are just having dinner to get reacquainted."

"Wear the black dress… the one you bought last month. It's pretty and looks classy."

Sheila held up a pearl and jeweled walking cane. "Even with this?"

"Especially with that one. It's all of *that*."

She struck a pose. "I figure if I have to use one—I might as well get a few blinged out ones. I'm still going to be cute."

Kiya chuckled. "Seriously Mom… in that dress, nobody will be paying attention to your cane. With or without a cane —you always keep it cute."

"I couldn't care less if they do," Sheila responded. "If I don't want to have to crawl around on the ground—I need it."

She put on the dress, paused in front of the standing mirror and stared at her reflection.

Kiya stood beside her. "You look so beautiful."

Sheila lovingly embraced her daughter. "Thank you."

"Do you want me to order a pizza or something for Gray?"

"No, Valerie prepared dinner before she left."

"The food at school sucks," Kiya stated. "I miss your cooking and Miss Val's."

"We can prep some meals for you."

"That would be great. I'm already tired of fast food. Right now, the last thing I want to see is another burger or taco."

Sheila chuckled. "I know you never tire of pizza."

"Naaw… that'll never happen, Mama."

"Sweetie, you should probably head back to campus," Sheila said. "Thanks for helping me get ready."

Picking up her purse and car keys, Kiya responded, "You look gorgeous. I wish I could see the professor's face when he sees you."

Sheila laughed. "I'll tell you all about it. Now get going."

Kiya hugged her. "I'll call you tomorrow, Mama."

"Text me to let me know you arrived safely to your dorm room."

"Yes ma'am…"

"I'm a bit overprotective. I know… I love you and Gray with my entire being. I can't lose either one of you."

"We feel the same way about you. We've already lost a set of parents. That was enough."

"Make sure to be aware of your surroundings."

"Like you always tell me… God is the ultimate when it comes to security. He's the best bodyguard we could have. I have my taser and pepper spray. I have the tools I learned in self-defense class, I'm observant and careful."

"Thank you for that gentle reminder, love."

Sheila escorted her daughter to the door. "Drive safe."

"Have fun tonight, Mama. I'll text you when I get back to the dorm. Love you…"

"Love you, too." She checked her reflection in the mirror in the foyer, then took a deep breath and exhaled softly. "Okay… I'm ready for this."

"Hello gorgeous…" he said as she opened the front door.

Nicholas awarded Sheila with a warm smile that made her knees weaken beneath her.

"It's a delight to see you again after all this time." His closely cropped hair was lightly peppered with gray. She noticed his intense, gray-colored gaze flick across her face, an amused expression drawing up the corners of his full, sensual mouth. The forty-three years he'd been on this earth were very good to him.

They embraced, then slowly moved apart.

"Thank you, Nicholas for the compliment." She knew he'd noticed the faint circles under her eyes and her slender, almost brittle-looking arms hidden beneath the sheer sleeves. She felt compelled to say, "I was sick a few weeks ago, and I lost quite a bit of weight. I'm much better now—just working to get my appetite back on track."

"You're still very beautiful."

Her mouth curved into an unconscious smile. "You're looking pretty good yourself," she responded. He looked very handsome in his designer suit. Sheila pretended not to notice the ripple of his muscles beneath the cloth as he escorted her to his car.

When his warm, gray eyes met hers, Sheila felt an intensity she couldn't describe in their depths. "I should've told you this a long time ago just how much I truly appreciate you."

"I really like your hair that way," Nicholas said.

Fingering a loc, she responded, "I stopped wearing weaves years ago. It was just too much for me to maintain. I found braids easier, then I transitioned to sister locs."

"I'm so glad we've reconnected," Nicholas said during the drive to the restaurant.

Sheila regarded him with curiosity. "Why is that?"

"I never stopped caring about you."

Her blood soared with unbidden memories. Although she tried to keep them pure and unsullied, one painful memory left a burning imprint on her. Sheila stared out the passenger window, then said, "Yet you moved on with another woman."

"Not really."

Sheila turned to meet his gaze. "Meaning?"

"I tried to move on, but I wasn't able to," he responded. "I couldn't keep you out of my head. I hope you won't lock me out of your life this time."

"Nicholas, I had to protect my heart."

"I understand."

"I need to know something," Sheila said. "If Kiya hadn't come to your office, would you have reached out?"

"Oh, I was definitely going to contact you," Nicholas assured her. "Your daughter just made it easier. I didn't want to just show up on your porch, but I would've…"

She laughed. "I actually believe you."

"You should because I'm being honest with you," Nicholas stated.

"You've always been straight with me. It's one of the things I love about you."

"Don't stop there. What else do you love?"

"That's all you're getting for now."

Sheila broke into a smile when he pulled into the parking lot of her favorite restaurant. "You remembered…"

"Of course," Nicholas responded. "I remember all of your favorites."

He got out and walked around the car to open the door for her.

"Why are you so quiet?" Nicholas asked when they were seated at a table ten minutes later.

"I don't know why, but this just feels surreal. I've missed you terribly. I was actually beginning to believe that I never thought I'd see you again."

"You could've reached out to me."

"I know." Sheila looked out the window at a couple of people approaching the entrance, then back at Nicholas. "I thought about it, but decided it was best to let you live your life. I also needed to live mine."

"You've always been in my thoughts."

She looked at him. "Even when you were dating someone else?"

Nicholas nodded. "That's why it didn't work out. You were still in my system. In my heart."

She cleared her throat, relaxing a little. "I should've apologized back then. I didn't mean to make you so unhappy when we were together. I wasn't thinking of anyone but myself. I was selfish."

"I bear some responsibility in what happened, Sheila." Nicholas reached over and took her hand in his own. "This time I'm not giving up on you."

She wanted desperately to believe him. Sheila was devastated when Nicholas ended their relationship. Her pain worsened when he told her that he'd met someone.

Sheila glanced around the restaurant. "It's been a while since I've been here."

"Really?"

"I always thought of you whenever I used to come, so I stopped eating here." Grinning, Sheila said, "It's so good to be back. *Thank you.*"

"You don't have to thank me, Sheila."

She laid her napkin across her lap. "I appreciate the effort you're putting forth, but I have to warn you—I need some time. I'm not going to just jump back into your arms, Nicholas. I was really hurt when we broke up."

He leaned forward, saying, "I understand."

His sexy grin was contagious.

Sheila's mouth curved into an unconscious smile.

"I truly missed that gorgeous smile of yours. When I look at those luscious lips of yours, all I think about is kissing you."

"Slow down, Nicholas," she interjected quickly with a slight wave of her hand. Sheila wanted him to kiss her, but she couldn't think about this right now.

"I can't help it."

Sheila chuckled. "You're so handsome… it would be too easy to get caught up in you again, but seriously. Let's try to take it a tiny bit slower. I need more time to process every-thing." She picked up her menu and pretended to study it although Sheila already knew what she would order.

Nicholas eyed his menu as well.

"Any idea what you're getting?" she asked.

"I'm thinking about the shrimp and grits. What about you?"

"I was thinking about ordering my regular, but I'm going to try something new. Maybe the crab Alfredo. I've heard that it's delicious."

A server approached to take their orders.

While they waited for their food to arrive, Nicholas and Sheila made small talk.

"Do you still have your properties?"

She nodded. "I do. I have six now. They're all rented but I

have a family leaving soon. I'm trying to decide if I want to keep the property or sell it."

"How's your mother doing?"

"She's good. Ma moved back to her house after I adopted Kiya and Gray. She was really homesick, and I wanted her to be happy. I hired a housekeeper, and I had my children, so I was fine with her going back to Frogmore."

"I'm going to have to visit Miss Essie one weekend."

"Oh, she would love that, Nicholas. She adores you."

"I feel the same way about her."

The server returned with their meals.

"Everything looks and smells wonderful," Sheila stated.

Nicholas agreed. He blessed the food before they sampled their meals.

"Oh, this is soo good," Sheila murmured. "You've got to try this."

This was just like old times for them—tasting each other's entrée.

"Here... try this," Nicholas said. "I know you don't like grits, but I promise you're going to love these. They cook them in chicken broth, garlic, and cheese."

Sheila decided to keep an open mind and tasted the spoonful he offered. "Oh wow... I could eat these, but I'd also have to have the shrimp, sausage, onion and peppers. Oh, and the bacon crumbles. I'll order this next time I come."

"The menu's changed a lot but I'm glad they kept a few of their staple items."

Sheila glanced around the restaurant. "I'm so glad we came here. I've really missed this place."

They talked and laughed while they ate. She hadn't laughed this much in a long time—at least not with someone she was dating. Sheila paused a second, trying to recall the last time she'd even gone on a date. She glanced at Nicholas.

This isn't a date. We're just reconnecting.

The thought brought a certain sadness with it, but Sheila quickly pushed it away. She was going to enjoy this evening and Nicholas's company. Regardless of what the future held for them—they would always be friends.

AT FIFTY-TWO YEARS OLD, Sheila was still a beautiful woman with long, thin locs and full, pouty lips. Nicholas had never seen her so thin, and it concerned him, but she was in good spirits.

Lingering looks, sensual smiles—all signs that something still fizzled between them. He'd longed to kiss her all evening and when he finally got the opportunity to capture her lips, Nicholas wasn't disappointed. Now that he'd tasted her full lips, he wanted more.

In truth, Nicholas wanted all of her.

Driving away now felt more like trying to put the cork back into a bottle of wine, but it was the only choice. Neither he nor Sheila was ready for anything more. Nicholas hadn't expected her to be so adamant about not rushing into a relationship. He knew she loved him still, but she wasn't willing to test the waters so soon. The old Sheila would've rushed back into his arms, but he respected the woman she'd come to

be. It was her newfound strength and all-to0-familiar stub-
born streak that continued to draw Nicholas to her.

He'd enjoyed the evening and looked forward to
spending more time with Sheila. Before he dropped her at
home, she'd invited him over for lunch tomorrow. Nicholas
quickly accepted the invitation.

He spent the rest of his drive home thinking of Sheila and
the life he wanted with her. Nicholas also wanted to let her
know that she was the muse for his current work-in-progress.
A smile tumbled from his lips as he thought about the
blinged out cane she'd had with her tonight. Sheila was still a
bit of a fashionista, even if she didn't think so.

It was true she'd changed over the years, but Nicholas
thought of it more as she'd matured. She was happy and
she'd settled into motherhood. He was proud of Sheila. She'd
finally embraced the person she was always meant to be.

Chapter 3

THAT KISS WAS EVERYTHING!

Sheila practically floated into the shower stall. She hummed softly as the water rained down on her body.

It was wonderful to have Nicholas back in her life. He was still the same handsome, caring man he was ten years ago. Those intense gray eyes hadn't changed nor that extremely sexy grin of his. During dinner, it was like the past ten years never happened. Their conversation was natural and comfortable.

Gray was standing in her bedroom door when Sheila walked out of the bathroom.

"When did you get home?" she asked.

"About ten minutes ago. Did you have a good time on your date?"

"It wasn't a date. Just dinner with an old friend." She sat down on the edge of her bed. "Do you have homework?"

"It was slow at work, so I was able to get it all done at the store," Gray responded.

"What did your manager have to say about this?"

"She's the one who suggested I do it." He came and sat down beside Sheila. "So, tell me about this writer dude. I know Kiya is fan girling all over him."

Sheila chuckled. "His name is Nicholas Washington—which you already know because I've seen you devouring his novels, too."

Gray shrugged in nonchalant. "I was curious. I wanted to see what the fuss is all about."

"And?"

"He's a good writer. I enjoyed his books." Gray lay back on the bed. "So, is he the same man you used to hang out with?"

"He is," Sheila responded. "He is still an honest, caring friend."

Sitting up, Gray inquired, "Why didn't you ever marry him?"

"That's a story for another time, my handsome son," Sheila murmured. "I'm a bit tired, so I'm going to get some rest. I brought dessert home for you."

"Are you feeling okay?" Gray asked.

"I'm fine, sweetie," she reassured him. "Just tired. There's nothing for you to worry about."

"Is Kiya coming home this weekend?"

"I don't think so. She was here earlier." Sheila glanced at her son. "You're missing your sister, huh?"

He nodded.

"Why don't you go grab your dessert and bring it up here? You can keep me company until I fall asleep."

"I'll be right back, Gray said, standing to his feet.

There were no words to describe the love she felt for Kiya and Gray. Although she didn't give birth them—they were undeniably her children in every way that mattered. She finally understood what it meant to have a family when she met Kiya, who was thirteen at the time and her eleven-year-old little brother.

THE NEXT AFTERNOON, Nicholas arrived at Sheila's house for lunch.

"I'm glad you're prompt because I'm hungry," Sheila announced. "I had some leftover chicken salad, so I thought I'd make sandwiches."

"Sounds great." He pointed to the walker. "I can order something if you're not feeling up to it."

"I'm fine, Nicholas. It's just one of those days when I need a little more assistance than usual. I'm not completely helpless."

Nicholas accompanied her to the kitchen.

Sheila opened the refrigerator and retrieved the container of chicken salad. "My housekeeper is running errands for me. I would've had everything ready before you came otherwise."

"It's fine. I have a couple of hours free before my next class."

She spread the chicken salad on slices of bread as Nicholas talked about the courses, he was teaching this semester.

He stood leaning against the counter, gesturing broadly with his hands. Nicholas raised his voice, as though lecturing to a class filled with students.

Sheila broke into a grin. "Alright Professor Washington."

He smiled. "I get carried away when I'm passionate about something."

"Kiya's so excited about your class." She handed a plate to him. "There's pickles and chips if you're interested."

"I'll take chips," Nicholas responded.

Nicholas noted the graceful way Sheila moved, despite the walker she used to stabilize her gait. He cleared his throat, determined to do this the right way. "I want you to know that I'm not going to rush you into a relationship. Take as much time as you need, sweetheart. I'm not going anywhere."

"I appreciate that," Sheila responded. "I'm sure you know that I still care deeply for you, Nicholas. That's never changed for me either. I wanted to forget you… I tried really hard, but my heart wouldn't let me."

"Is that why you had Kiya give me your number?"

She nodded. "I wanted to see you again, but I'm not going to let my feelings run rampart."

"I understand," Nicholas said. "I want to make it clear that I'm not here for games, Sheila. I came back to Charleston because I know what I want or maybe I should say *who* I want."

"I believe you," she responded. "But it's been a long time…"

"This time I'm not going anywhere, Sheila."

She smiled in response.

SHEILA WAS ACUTELY aware of the heat behind the smokey gray of his eyes, the tingle of desire that skittered across her skin, raising gooseflesh on her arms. "I'm not going to make it easy for you, Nicholas. You're going to have to work to get me back." She folded her arms beneath her breasts.

"If something is worth having, it's worth working hard to get," he suddenly stopped talking, his hands stopped moving.

Sheila stared to see if he'd stopped breathing.

Nicholas's eyes locked with hers.

She almost stopped breathing herself.

"What's wrong?" he inquired.

"You've made me remember all the good times we shared." Sheila took a bite of her chicken sandwich, hoping to dispel the undercurrent of desire in the room. Sheila had trouble making her feet move across the hardwood floors. She had to pass behind Nicholas, very close to him in the narrow passage between the sink and the entrance.

They sat down at the table in the breakfast nook to finish their lunch.

This is going to be harder than I thought. How can I resist

those sweet kisses of his? That look he gives me—the one where he can see clean through to my soul.

"Remembering the good time is not a bad thing."

"No, it's not," Sheila agreed. "I have a confession. My emotions are all over the place, Nicholas."

"I can say it's the same for me. The more time we spend together—the more comfortable we'll become with each other. We'll figure it out together." He bit into his sandwich, chewing slowly. "Did you really make this chicken salad? It's delicious."

Beaming with pride, Sheila responded, "Yes, I did. Valerie made it for us when she first came to work here. Gray loved it so much—I had to ask for the recipe. He loves chicken salad. I have to make it at least once a week."

"You might as well add me to the list. In fact, I'll buy the ingredients if you're willing to make me some."

"I'd be happy to, and you don't need to buy anything. When I make it this weekend, I'll just make enough for you, too. I'm really glad you liked it."

"I love chicken salad," Nicholas said. "It's one of my favorites but not everyone can make it like this."

After lunch, he had to return to the university.

"Thank you for a delicious lunch and fantastic company. I'll call you later tonight."

The memory of what life was like before Nicholas struck Sheila. A period when she felt happiness was beyond her reach, fear that she would never find love and acceptance.

When she was first diagnosed with MS, Sheila felt life

hadn't been fair to her. However, multiple sclerosis changed her life in a positive way despite some of its challenges.

When Nicholas hugged her before leaving the house, Sheila felt the strength and rock hardness of his chest, even through the fabric of his coat.

He moved his hands up to gently circle her throat, then his thumbs traced the line of her jaw and, gently, the outline of her lips.

Sheila closed her eyes. Not to keep back tears, but to keep Nicholas from seeing what his touch was doing to her. Her heart sped up; her pulse pounded in her ears. She couldn't breathe.

He kissed her and the tremor when his lips met hers went through Sheila from head to toe. Nicholas must have felt it, too, because he stiffened and made a low sensuous growl deep in his throat.

His kiss deepened, became more demanding, and Sheila felt herself respond to the chemistry that still existed between them.

"I have to go, sweetheart."

She wanted more than anything to lift her fingers to his lips; to trace the line of his jaw, but she stuck her hands inside her pockets instead. "I know," she whispered.

Her time with Nicholas had come to an end. He had to return to the campus to teach another class. Sheila refused to acknowledge why it made her sad as she walked him to the door. Or why a sense of sadness clung to her, refusing to let go after she'd said goodbye.

Chapter 4

NICHOLAS LAY in bed that night thinking about how soft Sheila's hand had felt in his and how fragile she'd felt in his arms; how it felt to kiss her full, pouty lips.

He wasn't going to just let Sheila walk out of his life a second time. But he couldn't deny that the idea of them together was scary; especially since she was now a mother. Nicholas was a bit hesitant to get attached to Kiya and Gray, but he couldn't turn away now. He didn't just return to Charleston to teach at the university—he also came back reclaim Sheila's heart.

Nicholas had to give it one more attempt to make their relationship work. He didn't want to live out the rest of his life wondering what if...

He plumped up the pillows behind him, then settled back to review homework papers. This was definitely not his idea of the perfect ending to the evening, but it wasn't bad either.

Nicholas pushed away his thoughts of Sheila so he could concentrate on his grading assignments. He took solace that he would have a chance to see her tomorrow.

Since his return, Nicholas hadn't paid his long-time friend Tori a visit. He wasn't sure how she would feel about his involvement with Sheila, but he didn't care.

Tori was happily married and had three beautiful children. He didn't have a child but like Tori, he wanted to share his life with his soulmate.

"NICHOLAS HEY...," Tori Madison greeted when he strolled through the double doors of the bookstore. "I was wondering when you were going to grace us with a visit."

"I needed to get settled in my place, then prepare for my position at the university."

She walked around the counter and embraced him. "I'm so glad you're back. I've missed you."

"I missed you, too. How are the kids?"

"They're great," Tori responded. "So is Jake."

Nicholas smiled. "How are things with the business? I know he's had his hands full since Sheila is more of a consultant now."

"It's gotten better," she said. "He's made Marla a partner."

A woman entered through the doors of the bookstore. "Nicholas... I'd heard you were back."

"Yep." He smiled at Tori's cousin and business partner, Charlene. "I'm here to stay."

"Have you talked to Sheila?"

Nicholas wasn't surprised by Tori's question. She knew he still harbored feelings for her. "Yeah, I have. We actually had dinner last night and lunch earlier today."

"How is she doing?" Tori inquired. She appeared to be genuinely concerned.

"Pretty good. She has good and bad days as you can imagine. She doesn't let MS stop her from being an amazing mother."

"I'd heard she adopted a pair of siblings after they lost their parents."

"She did," Nicholas responded. "Kiya's actually a student of mine."

"Oh really?" Tori uttered. "That's pretty convenient."

"She's a gifted writer and she applied through the program like all the other students. I had no idea who her mother was until she came by my office and introduced herself."

"Nicholas, I hope you won't get upset with me, but I have to ask... did you come back here for Sheila? I know how much you love her."

"She's part of the reason," he confessed.

"How does she feel about it?" Tori questioned.

"We're taking it one day at a time."

"Are you sure about letting her back into your life like this? You know her history—what she's capable of... you know what she did to me."

"Yeah, I am, Tori. Sheila's not the same person you remember," Nicholas stated. "She's changed."

"You've been gone for five years. I'm just saying…"

"When was the last time you saw her?"

"It's been a while—maybe eight or nine years," Tori responded. "The last time I saw her was when one of the employees passed away. She came to the funeral. Sheila and I will never be friends, but you're like a brother to me. I just want you to be happy, Nicholas."

"I'm good, Tori."

She smiled. "I'm glad."

"I hope you're planning to autograph some of your books," Charlene interjected. "People love seeing your signature."

Nicholas chuckled. "Of course. I'd be honored. I'm glad people are still buying them."

Tori smiled. "You're a wonderful storyteller."

"I can't believe you're still single," Charlene stated. "I have a really good friend who also happens to be a huge fan of your books. It would make her day if she could meet you for lunch or dinner…"

"Give it up, cousin," Tori said. "Nicholas's heart belongs to Sheila."

"You're *kidding*. She's like ten or eleven years older than you, right?"

"She's only nine years older,' he responded.

Charlene opened her mouth to say something, but Tori stopped her by saying, "Let it go…"

She glanced at her cousin. "Did you forget everything she did to you and Jake? Because I haven't." Her eyes strayed to

Nicholas. "Things didn't work out with you and Sheila the first time. Why are you so eager to go running back to her?"

"Because I love her. We're not the same people we were ten years ago, Charlene. Frankly, I'm disappointed in you. You of all people know that none of us are perfect. We make mistakes, bad choices—whatever you want to call it. But it doesn't mean we never grow up. It doesn't mean that we're not deserving of a second chance."

"Nicholas's right," Tori interjected. "Charlene, why don't you get the books for him to sign?"

When her cousin walked off, she said, "Sorry about that."

Nicholas shrugged in nonchalance. "It's fine. You know I've never been one to care what others think. I will make up my own mind about a person."

"You're right about that." Tori paused a moment, then said, "I see you're still not crazy about my husband."

"Jake doesn't care for me," Nicholas responded. "As long as he makes you happy—I'm cool with him."

"We're very happy. I love him more and more each day. Jake and I are really good."

"That's all that matters."

Tori agreed. "You're right, Nicholas."

"I hope you know what you're doing," Charlene interjected.

"I know exactly what I'm doing. It's something I should've done a long time ago."

A DAY LATER, the doorbell rang just as Sheila was about to order something for dinner. Valerie's sister wasn't feeling well, so she gave her housekeeper the day off. She left the menu sitting on the kitchen counter and went to answer the door.

Sheila opened it quickly, expecting to find a driver delivering a package, but instead she found Nicholas standing there. Her eyes widened in surprise. "Hey… I wasn't expecting to see you tonight."

He was holding two boxes of pizza and a six-pack of Pepsi. "I hope you don't mind, but I thought I would bring dinner by tonight. Over the phone, you sounded like you were really exhausted earlier, and I knew your housekeeper wasn't here to cook."

"I don't mind at all," she said with a grin. "I'm actually relieved. I was about to order food. Kiya's picking up Gray from the mall. His car is in the shop so they should be here shortly."

"What happened to his car?" He followed her to the kitchen.

"His brakes need replacing."

Nicholas sat the pizza boxes on the counter. "I have Hawaiian style pizza and the other is veggie."

"How did you know?" Sheila asked.

"I asked Kiya earlier."

"How is she doing in your class?"

"Great."

Nicholas's sudden arrival was a blessing in disguise because she wasn't feeling her best either. Sheila ventured to the dining room with a stack of paper plates and napkins.

"We're home," Kiya called out, entering the house from the garage. "Gray found some shoes he likes and there were some great sales on clo..." She stopped short when she saw Nicholas. "Oh... hey Professor Washington. I didn't know you were here."

"Nicholas brought dinner," Sheila announced. "And you can quit acting like you're surprised. He already mentioned that he'd asked you about dinner."

"I smell pizza," Gray bellowed, his arms laden with shopping bags. "I hope there's some Hawaiian style in one of those boxes."

"There certainly is," Nicholas stated. "I know it's your mom's favorite."

"Mine, too."

"I hope you didn't spend all of your paycheck on shoes."

Gray held up his shopping bags. "I didn't. I only bought one pair this time. The other bags are clothes for school. I think I'm good for a few months."

"I'm sure," Sheila responded with a chuckle.

After washing their hands, Kiya and her brother joined them at the table, eating pizza and participating in light conversation.

This was the first man who'd come around her children in three years. She'd dated someone briefly—too brief to even think about.

Although Gray and Kiya were polite and engaging, she knew they were studying Nicholas, observing his every action. It was kind of him to bring dinner tonight. He'd somehow known she wasn't feeling well. Nicholas coming to her aid wasn't surprising—it's just that Sheila didn't expect him to be this supportive upon his return to Charleston.

When he looked at her across the table with the heat of attraction in his eyes, Sheila felt a rush of heat flow through her body.

Chapter 5

AFTER SEVERAL SLICES of pizza and a TV movie, Gray went upstairs, while Kiya quickly got up and cleared the table, carrying the empty plates to the trash can.

"Would you like another Pepsi, or would you prefer to upgrade to red or white wine?" Sheila asked Nicholas.

"I'm fine with the soda." Nicholas got up from the table and carried the box with leftover pizza slices into the kitchen.

"Are you planning on going back to the campus tonight?" Sheila asked her daughter.

"I'm staying here tonight. Gray needs some help with Statistics." Kiya wiped down the counter, then asked, "Mama, would you like a cup of tea?"

"Yes, thank you, sweetie," Sheila replied, then explained, "I suffer from a little insomnia."

"So do I," Nicholas said. "Sometimes I do my best writing in the middle of the night."

"I cook," she responded. "I can't just lay in bed when I can't sleep so sometimes, I go to the kitchen, make meals and put them in the freezer. It helps me focus on something other than my pain."

Sheila gestured toward the door. "Let's sit out on the patio," she said. "It's a nice evening and I don't often get the chance to enjoy it anymore."

They went out of the sliding glass door to a covered patio. Sheila had the seating area with a table, and six outdoor chairs with cushions. She lit the citronella candle in the center of the table and sat down with a soft sigh.

"Are you in pain?" Nicholas asked out of concern.

"I'm fine."

Kiya walked out of the house with two cups of honey and chamomile tea. "I figured you could use some as well, Professor."

"Thank you," he responded while accepting the mug.

"You have two great kids," Nicholas stated when Kiya went back into the house.

"I do," Sheila agreed.

She took a sip of her tea.

"That's the one regret I have... I've always wanted a family."

"I remember. You'd make a wonderful father."

He smiled ruefully. "I always thought so, too."

"It's not too late for you, Nicholas. I'm sure it wouldn't be too much of a challenge for you to find a wife—a young wife."

"I don't want a young wife, Sheila. There's only one

woman I want to be with. I just need to know if she'll have me."

"Are you talking about me?"

"Yeah."

"After everything I put you through—you want to be with me?"

Nicholas nodded. "Sheila... I've a lot of time to think about this and even though I tried to move on without you—I couldn't. You're the one woman for me."

"Are you sure about this?"

"I am. But I need to know how you feel."

Sheila placed a hand to her chest. "Give me a minute..."

After a moment, she said, "Nicholas, you know how much I care for you. It's why I cut off all communication when you started seeing someone. It broke my heart."

"She's not an issue, Sheila. There's nothing standing in our way this time. We're both in a better space at this stage of our lives. There's something I need to ask you. I know we're not rushing into a relationship but are you interested in starting over with me?"

"Wow..." Sheila murmured. "I wasn't expecting those words to come out of your mouth."

"We're not as young as we used to be. I feel like we've wasted enough time. Don't you?"

Sheila agreed. "Yes, we have, but Nicholas... we need to get to know each other all over again. The other thing is that I don't want to be a burden."

"You've never be a burden."

Her eyes widened as she listened to him speak. Nicholas took her hand in his, and she didn't pull away.

"It's been a while, so I want to get to know the woman you are now. Will you let me?"

Sheila's lips softly parted as she nodded. "Yes," she said softly.

Nicholas closed the gap between them, his lips pressing gently against her own. His hand caressed her cheek, pulling her closer. "I've really missed you."

"I missed you, too."

He looked into Sheila's eyes, then whispered. "I'd better go. It's getting pretty late."

There was a momentary expression of disappointment on her face, but it quickly disappeared, replaced with a smile. "Okay," Sheila responded. "Thanks for coming over tonight and bringing pizza. The kids and I really appreciate it."

Nicholas stood and they made their way back into the house.

Hovering by the front door, he hesitated to leave but knew that he should. "If you're feeling up to it, why don't we go to the park on Saturday. We can have a fun, relaxing day together."

"Sure. I'll let you know by Friday. Hopefully, I'll feel much better than I do right now."

He kissed her on the forehead. "Get some rest, sweetheart."

"Thanks again for dinner tonight."

'My pleasure." Nicholas slipped out the door and went out to his car.

Sheila watched from the doorway as he left. She waved as he backed out of the driveway.

He still worried about her, probably more than he should, but no matter how many times Nicholas tried in the past—he couldn't stay away. He knew without a doubt Sheila was the one woman who owned his heart.

KIYA MET Sheila at her bedroom door. "Looks like my professor still has feelings for you."

"He said as much."

"What did you say?"

"I told him that I wasn't going to rush back into his arms. I need to think about everything."

"What's there to think about, Mama?" Kiya asked as she turned down the bed. "I can tell you're still crazy about him."

"I just want to enjoy this time with Nicholas. I don't want to rush into a relationship and things end badly."

"You can't think like that. Be *positive*."

"Honey, I am. I'm just protecting my heart. I made a lot of mistakes in the past, Kiya and I didn't go about things in the right way. I'm going to be smarter this time around. There's stuff you don't know about me but you're my daughter and I don't want you to make the same stupid choices I made."

After a short pause, Sheila said, "You and Gray lost both your parents in a horrific way. Before the two of you came into my life, I'd always believed that my life sucked. I was born in that same four-room shanty in Frogmore where your grandmother lives. My father was my world… one day he left us and never looked back. He started another family and had a great life while my mother turned to pills and alcohol, leaving me to take care of us both. I was an ugly duckling and bullied in school. Despite the hell that was my life, I studied hard and worked two jobs to go to college. I was determined to have the life I always dreamed of—no matter the cost. Then I met Jake Madison who became my study partner and only friend really. He and Tori were dating at the time, but I did everything I could to win his affection, including spending thousands on plastic surgery and the creation of Madison-Moore. Outside of my father, Jake was the only man I'd ever loved—they both rejected me."

She eyed her daughter. "I tried to break up Jake's marriage. I wasn't a nice person." Sheila wiped away a tear.

Kiya hugged her mother. "You just wanted to be loved. Mama, you're not that same person anymore. You always tell me not to live in the past. You can't either. The Sheila Moore I know is a kind and loving woman. Gray and I used to have to hide in our bedrooms when my dad would beat my mom. He used to always threaten to kill her. I guess she got tired of it because she sent us to her friend's house. The police say she shot him while he was sleeping, then killed herself." Kiya's eyes filled with tears. "I guess she thought she'd go to prison, and she didn't want that. Gray and I thought we'd be in the system until we aged out, but then you came into our lives."

"When I heard what happened on the news, I felt this fierce need to protect you and your brother—I didn't want you to grow up like me… angry and bitter. I wanted you and

Gray to know that someone cared, and you wouldn't have to feel alone in the world. I prayed that I'd be able to adopt you and your brother. I didn't ask God for anything else, not financial security, happiness, or the love of a man. I wanted to be your mother."

"You saved us, Mama. You put us in therapy... we never thought we could live the way we do now. You just dropped some real money on school clothes for me and Gray. Our parents struggled and relied on the government. You're a partner with Madison, Moore & Parks Creative Visual Solutions, Inc.; a company that's global. You spend time with us and make sure we're okay when I know some days it's hard for you to get out of bed. I still remember our second Christmas with you," Kiya said. "You weren't feeling too good, so Grandma brought all the gifts to your room, and we spent the day in there with you. The room was all decorated and Christmas music was playing in the background... we even got to have dinner in your room with you. It was really nice."

"I couldn't ruin the holiday for you."

"Mama, what are you scared of?" Kiya asked. "Professor Washington wants to be with you. He could've worked at any other school, but he came back here."

"It's really not Nicholas I'm worried about, Kiya. I don't want to mess this up a second time."

"Mama, you won't... Professor Washington loves you. Just give him a chance."

"You really think I should?" Sheila asked.

Kiya nodded. "Yeah, I do. I love the way you are when

you're with him. Your smile is brighter… your eyes—they light up whenever you look at Professor Washington."

"I've never loved anyone as much as I love Nicholas. Not even Jake Madison."

"Then you need to tell him. Don't waste any more time, Mama. Gray and I will never be able to get back all the years I've lost with my mom because of the choice she made. It's a different situation, but kinda the same. You want to be with him—*tell him*."

Sheila embraced Kiya. "I love you, my beautiful daughter."

"I love you more, Mama."

The fall weather held a trace of brisk air, prompting Sheila to rub her arms to ward off the chill. She continued standing at the window, exploring a future with Nicholas. He possessed all of the qualities she's always wanted in a man. Trust and honesty were of extreme importance to him, and she felt the same way. No relationship could work without them.

"I don't want to lose Nicholas," she whispered to the empty room. "This time I have to be completely honest with him."

COOL, moist air washed in as Nicholas left Sheila's house, his headlights gleamed off wet asphalt as he drove home. The rain had stopped sometime before but the air smelled fresh with the scent of late summer in Charleston.

It was his favorite kind of night, a night of great company, pizza, games, with the smooth sounds of Miles Davis playing in the background. He sighed, driving past the half-dozen darkened shops that comprised the city's lively downtown.

Nicholas returned alone to the empty three-bedroom townhome he'd bought when he'd moved back to Charleston.

On nights like this he often wondered what it would be like to have someone to welcome him home—to come home to Sheila. It was a tantalizing thought, but he refused to dwell on it for long. Nicholas didn't want to get his hopes up in the event things didn't go the way he wanted them to go. She was scared to open her heart fully to him at the moment, but he was determined to find a way to break down the walls.

Deep down, he wasn't really worried because he knew in his heart what he'd heard God say when he prayed about his desire to reunite with Sheila. Nicholas glanced at the king-sized bed and smiled. He wouldn't be sleeping alone too much longer. He walked over to his dresser and picked up the small black velvet box. When the time was right, he planned to ask Sheila to marry him.

Chapter 6

NICHOLAS WAS on his way over to the house at her request.

Sheila felt like a nervous teen experiencing her first real crush. She didn't know why she was so anxious, but once she got everything out, she could relax.

She stole a peek at the clock as she paced. Nicholas was due to arrive at any moment. Sheila didn't like exposing her vulnerability, but he deserved to know the truth.

The sound of someone knocking interrupted her musings.

Sheila opened the door to let Nicholas inside.

He was instantly concerned. "Are you feeling okay?"

"Babe, I'm fine... I just needed to talk to you and if I waited—I might talk myself out of having this conversation."

They sat down in the living room.

"I'm listening,' Nicholas said when she sat down beside him.

"I've been thinking a lot about us," Sheila said. "I know

that I told you I didn't want to rush into anything, but I also don't want to waste whatever time we have left, Nicholas."

"What are you telling me?"

"I only want you. You're the man I love. We have a chance for a do over and I'd like very much to start fresh. Love is a blessing, and I don't want to just casually toss it to the side. When you left, it really hurt. Then when you told me you'd met someone... you know it's funny how quickly your heart can break. When I realized it was truly over between us, I felt it snap, just like that. There wasn't any pain really. I suppose I was numb to it, but not long after... the agony of losing you hit me hard."

"I was also hurt, Sheila. I felt like I'd lost a part of my soul. That's when I knew without a doubt that we belong together. This time nothing or no one will come between us."

She gave a slight nod. "My heart belongs to you."

He kissed her. Nicholas' hands were still warm and strong, his touch sure and confident. In his arms, Sheila absorbed his warmth and his unconditional love.

"It's about time you two made it official," Kiya said from the doorway.

Sheila hadn't heard her daughter come into the house. "What are you doing here?"

"I came to pick up Gray. We're going to eat and see a movie. He's been wanting some sibling time."

"I take it that you're okay with me seeing your mom," Nicholas stated.

"I'm thrilled about it," Kiya responded. She propped her

body against one of the accent chairs. "And don't worry—I don't expect any special treatment in class."

Sheila chuckled.

"I'm glad to hear it," Nicholas responded with a grin.

"Just one more thing… don't do anything to hurt my mother. She's deserving of real love."

"I agree."

"I'd better go upstairs to get my brother. That boy don't know anything about being on time."

"Kiya's very protective of you, I see."

"So is Gray," Sheila responded. "Although I didn't give birth to them, they are very much my heartbeats. I can't imagine life without them."

"I hope they'll accept me as a father figure one day."

"I don't see that being a problem," Sheila said with a grin. "They both really like you, Nicholas. They know how much I love you."

"I know they're not young children, but I hope in the near future to adopt them—I'd like to give them my name. Presuming you will also have my name."

Sheila kissed him gently on the lips. "That's a very real possibility Mr. Washington."

NICHOLAS ENTERED HIS HOUSE, a huge smile on his face. He was delighted by Sheila's decision to give their relationship a second chance. However, he couldn't immerse himself in celebrating right now. He had a stack of English papers that needed to be graded.

Shortly after eight o'clock, his cell phone rang.

Nicholas didn't recognize the number on the caller ID.

He answered, saying, "This is Nicholas Washington."

"Nick, it's me."

Frowning in confusion, he asked, "Me who?"

"Diana. Your former *wife*. Surely, I'm not that forgettable."

"It's been a while," Nicholas responded without emotion. "Over eighteen years."

"Well, from the looks of it, life has been pretty great to you."

Without preamble, Nicholas questioned, "Diana, why are you calling me now? The last time I saw you—we were in divorce court." When she'd walked out on him back then, it left an aching, empty chasm in the middle of his soul. It had taken a while, but he eventually got over her and moved on with his life.

"I know that I didn't handle our split the right way, she said, "But I'm hoping we can get past that because there's something we need to talk about."

"What would that be?" Nicholas couldn't imagine what his ex-wife wanted to discuss after all this time.

"I guess the first thing I should do is formally apologize for the way things ended between us. I was wrong and I'm sorry."

"That was a long time ago," Nicholas stated. "We've both moved on."

"Still, you deserved better," Diana responded. "I was young and foolish. I didn't know what I wanted."

"As I stated earlier. Both of us have moved on with our lives. We're good, so I'm not sure where you're going with this."

"Nick, I left you because I discovered I was pregnant. I was afraid because I was cheating on you."

He shook his head in confusion. "You left me three years before you had a child or that's what I heard."

"I was pregnant when I left you. Three years later, I had another daughter, but she was stillborn. I was pregnant with her when Steve and I got married. I had a set of twin boys fifteen months later."

"Why are you unburdening yourself now? There's really no need for all this. It's been almost nineteen years."

"Please hear me out."

"Okay. I'm listening."

"I choose Steve because of the baby," Diana said. She paused a moment, then said, "I *thought* he was the father."

Nicholas didn't respond.

"Did you hear me?"

"Yes, I heard you, Diana but I still don't understand why you're telling me all this."

She let out a sigh, then said, "Nick, you have a daughter. Zoe isn't Steve's child. She's yours."

"Excuse me?"

"Nick, I really thought she was his child."

"Why didn't you just tell me you were pregnant, Diana? What did you think I would do?" Nicholas asked. "Is it because I would've demanded a paternity test? We were still sleeping together up until you left."

"I was sure she couldn't be yours because of the timing. I thought she was conceived while you were in Brunswick taking care of your mother. You were gone for two weeks, remember. I just couldn't bear to see the hurt I inflicted on you. I was a coward."

"Does Steve know the truth?"

"Yes, he does," Diana responded. "We just found out recently and as you can imagine, he's devastated. He feels like I lied to him. Right now, he's furious with me."

Nicholas remained quiet.

"I'd told him that you and I weren't having sex back then," Diana stated. "He wanted me all to himself."

"So, you *were* lying to him, too. A paternity test could've cleared all this up a long time ago. We were struggling financially back then," Nicholas said. "Steve Winston comes from money, and you wanted the lifestyle that comes with it—that's why you hid the fact that you were pregnant. You made sure I never found out about her—you knew I'd want to have a paternity test."

"What do you want me to say, Nicholas? That I'm a horrible person? Trust me, *I know it.*"

"Have you told your daughter the truth?" he inquired.

"She's *our* daughter and yes, I have. I was left with no choice. Yesterday, Steve announced that he wants a divorce. He says he can't be around me or my daughter. He's threatened to embarrass me in court if I objected to him having custody of our boys. I know he's already met someone else."

She paused a moment, then said, "I'm sure you're thinking that I'm getting exactly what I deserve."

"I wasn't thinking that at all," Nicholas responded. "I'm still trying to digest the fact that I may have a daughter."

"You *do* have one, and she's smart and beautiful," Diana said. "She's a freshman in college. Zoe wants to be an accountant."

"That's great."

"This has been very confusing for Zoe and Steve's not making it any easier. Can you believe he wants me to pay him back for all the money he spent on my daughter? He's no longer paying for her education. I've had to withdraw Zoe from school."

"It sounds like he's hurt and angry. I can certainly understand why, but I wouldn't punish the child."

"I didn't do this on purpose."

"I can't say I believe that, but this is something you should be discussing this with your husband, Diana."

"Every time I try… he's r-rude and treats me like dirt, but what I can't deal with is the way he's treating my d-daughter." Her voice broke and she started sobbing.

Nicholas wasn't swayed by her tears. A wave of anger washed over him. Diana played a game which affected everyone including her daughter. He couldn't understand why she kept his daughter from him all these years. Was she that greedy for money? Was Zoe really his child?

"I just want to get her away from here," Diana said, cutting into his thoughts. "I was thinking of coming to

Charleston. Zoe really wants to meet you. If you don't mind, we can come next weekend if that's okay."

"Sure," Nicholas responded. "I'd like to meet her, too."

When they hung up, he sat staring off into space.

I have a daughter.

———

SHEILA WAS SURPRISED to hear from Nicholas so early the next day. She figured he would be in the middle of teaching a class.

"How are you feeling?" he inquired.

"I'm feeling so much better today," she said, "but you don't sound like you're okay. Did something happen?"

"Why do you ask?"

"Nicholas, I can hear it in your voice. I can tell something's weighing on you. What's going on?"

"Do you mind if I come by in about an hour? I'd like for us to talk in person."

Sheila wasn't sure what to think but wasn't going to let her mind go to the negative. "Sure. If you have time, I'll make a light lunch."

"Thanks. I should be there around twelve-thirty."

She knew him well enough to know that something was troubling Nicholas. He needed someone with whom to share his troubles and Sheila was honored that he'd chosen her.

He arrived promptly a half hour after twelve.

Sheila had prepared a Cobb salad with grilled chicken for lunch.

Nicholas greeted her with a kiss. "Thanks for allowing me to drop in on you like this. I really needed to talk to someone."

"I have to confess that I'm shocked you came to me and not Tori."

"Tori has her hands full with the children and the bookstore," he responded. "Besides, I only want to share this with you for right now."

Nicholas picked up the plates and carried them to the table for Sheila who was using her cane as support.

Once they were seated, Nicholas blessed the food, then sampled his meal. "This is delicious."

Sheila smiled. "Thank you. If I'd had more time, I could've prepared a real meal."

"You cook?"

Laughing, she gave a slight nod. "When I realized I wanted to be a mother—I actually had to learn how to cook. I don't always have the energy, but when I feel up to it—I enjoy it. I've learned how to make a lot of quick and easy salads; casseroles and I love my crock pot."

"I noticed you've also changed in the way you used to dress," Nicholas stated. "You've never been a jean and a tee-shirt kind of woman."

Sheila leaned back in her chair grinning. "You're right. There was a time when I wouldn't be caught dead in a pair of jeans. When I graduated college—I vowed to never wear denim again in life. Now they're my favorite."

"You look great in everything you wear, Sheila."

"I know you didn't come here to discuss my choice of

clothing. What's happened? Is everything okay with your family?"

"They're all fine. However, my family has increased recently."

"That's great news. Isn't it?"

"Yes, I suppose so," Nicholas commented.

She studied his expression. What happened?"

"My ex-wife called me last night."

"Oh wow…" Sheila murmured. "She just happened to call you out of the blue after all this time—what did she want? How did she even find you?"

"Probably from my mom or sister," he responded. "Diana would've reached out to them if she wanted to locate me."

"But why now?"

Nicholas took Sheila's hand in his own. "Diana informed me that the reason she left was because she was pregnant—she'd been cheating on me. However, she recently discovered that the child is actually mine and not her husband's."

Sheila gasped in shock. It took a few minutes for her to process what he was saying. When she found her voice, she asked, "How do you feel about this?"

"I'm not sure," Nicholas responded with a shrug. "I've always wanted to be a father. To find out after eighteen years that I have a daughter… if I'd known about the pregnancy, I would've insisted on a paternity test."

"You had no idea she was seeing someone?"

Nicholas shook his head no. "I was oblivious. When she left, I just figured she wasn't happy with me. She didn't marry Steve Winston until three years later. I knew she was pregnant then, but I'd heard nothing about Zoe or even that there was an older child. But then, it's not like I was interested in what was going on with her. We were over, so I focused on my writing."

"The good news is that you have a daughter. I'm sure she's beautiful."

"I'm still trying to process all this."

"Does she know about you? Your daughter."

Nicholas nodded. "She wants to meet me. Diana wants to bring Zoe to Charleston next weekend."

"I see." Sheila wasn't exactly thrilled over the fact that his ex-wife had suddenly reappeared in Nicholas's life, but she and their daughter was a package deal. He couldn't have one without dealing with the other.

"Sheila, none of this changes the way I feel about you or that I want your children in my life."

She smiled. "You know they really like you." Sheila had recently fantasized about Nicholas being part of their family —being a father to her kids.

"I'm glad to hear that." Nicholas met her gaze. "I have to admit I wasn't sure how well you were going to take this news."

"I keep telling you that I'm not the same woman you left all those years ago," Sheila said. "Remember the Bible you gave me?" When Nicholas nodded, she continued. "It's worn from my studying, highlighting, and taking notes…the Father and I have spent a lot of time together and in getting to know His character—I've been forever changed."

"I can see that," he responded.

"Nicholas, this is a good thing," Sheila said with a smile. "You've always wanted to be a dad and now you have an opportunity. I'm very happy for you. I really love being a mom..."

"I want you with me when I meet Zoe," Nicholas announced.

"Are you sure about this?"

"Yeah..."

"Maybe you two should just have this moment together," Sheila suggested. She didn't know anything about Nicholas's ex-wife, but the timing of all this made her suspicious. However, she didn't voice her thoughts. Sheila decided to just wait until she met Diana face-to-face.

"You're a very important part of my life. From now on, we tackle everything as a couple."

"How do you feel about seeing your ex-wife again?"

Nicholas shrugged in nonchalance. "I don't have any feelings one way or the other. I'm just interested in seeing if this girl is my daughter."

"So, you do have doubts?"

"I do. Why *now*? I intend to keep an open mind, but none of this really makes sense to me."

"Maybe she really did believe that the child wasn't yours, Nicholas. I'm not defending her by any means, but it's possible."

"I've wanted this for so long..." he shook his head. "I've missed out on the last eighteen years of this girl's life and I'm angry about it."

"You have every right to be," Sheila stated. "I'd feel the same way, babe. What your ex did… she was wrong."

"I've really got to work on my heart before they arrive next weekend. I feel robbed."

Sheila hugged him. "I'm so sorry. Babe, try to focus on the positive in this situation—you have a daughter. Don't think about your ex-wife. She doesn't matter at this point."

"You're right about that," Nicholas uttered. "The only other thing that matters is the truth."

"Once you see her, your heart will recognize the truth. If not, you can always order a DNA test."

Chapter 7

"GOOD NEWS...YOU'RE gonna meet your daddy next weekend. I spoke with him earlier and he was so excited," Diana announced when her daughter walked into their hotel room in Newark, New Jersey.

Zoe broke into a wide grin. "Really? *The Nicholas Washington* really wants to see me."

She chuckled. "Of course. He's your father, Zoe. Why wouldn't he want to get to know his own daughter?"

"Mama, why is it that you never once suspected that he was my dad?"

Zoe's question caught Diana off guard. It took her a moment to respond, "I was young, and I just assumed Steve was your father. I don't know why... maybe because I was so in love with him."

"What happened between you and Nicholas?" Zoe asked. "Why did you have an affair with Dad... I mean Steve?"

"I was crazy in love with Nick, but he was always work-ing. When he *was* home—he was working on his book. Steve and I just clicked when I started working as his father's administrative assistant. It started off with us just being friends, but then things changed. We went to lunch one day and he told me he was in love with me. I was really lonely..."

"Why didn't Grandpa Winston like you?"

"George didn't think I was good enough for his son. He wanted Steve to marry some bougie socialite, but he fell in love with me. He'd threatened to cut him out of his will, but Steve didn't think he'd really do it—he was the only son." Diana picked up one of the throw pillows and held it close to her. "That old man meant it though. He left everything to Martha."

Her father-in-law died last month. She and Steve were shocked by the news that not only did George leave every-thing to her sister-in-law, but Martha was also the new CEO and president of Winston Electronics, the position they'd always assumed Steve would hold upon his father's death.

Diana was furious over the turn her life had taken. And she was disappointed in the way Steve just folded—he didn't attempt to fight his sister for power, money or even challenge the will. She'd given up everything to be with him. At the time, Steve seemed to have more going on than Nicholas. She'd never been so wrong.

"Zoe, I need to tell you something," Diana said. "When we leave, we're not coming back here, but say nothing to Steve."

"What about the boys?"

"They really want to stay with their father," she responded. "Right now, I have to figure out what to do next and it's not fair to disrupt their lives. It's not right that you must withdraw from school. I can't believe Steve would do this to you."

"You keep telling me that Dad… eh Steve doesn't want a relationship with me anymore. He's called me a few times since we left the house. Do you think I should call him back?"

"No. He just probably wants to talk trash about me," Diana uttered. "Just forget about that man. It's time for you to focus on building a relationship with your biological father."

"Where are we staying in Charleston?" Zoe asked.

"With your father, of course," Diana stated. "Just leave it to me."

"Mama, are you sure about this? Maybe Steve just needs some time to cool off. You two have been married almost sixteen years. As for school, I can apply for financial aid to help with my tuition."

"I'm not gonna have you saddled with student loans. Your father teaches at a prestigious university. I'm sure you can go there for free or at least at a deeply discounted rate. I know Nick…he'll make sure you get a good education."

"I don't think we should expect him to do something like that—the man doesn't even know me."

"He's your father. He owes you, Zoe."

"Mama, we can't expect Nicholas to just open up his wallet when he sees me. It's not right. Besides, I don't want him to feel like he's obligated to pay for my education when he didn't know anything about me."

Diana met her gaze. "Girl, Nick owes you eighteen years of child support. I intend to collect." If she'd known Nicholas would become a bestselling author with almost fifty books published and several major movies under his belt—Diana most likely wouldn't have strayed into the arms of another man. She never thought his writing would go anywhere. How wrong she'd been.

I was his one true love. Getting Nicholas back should be easy.

The thought brought a smile to her lips.

DIANA AND ZOE were due to arrive any moment now.

"You're pacing," Sheila told Nicholas. "Babe, just relax... Zoe's going to love you."

"You really think so?"

"I do," she responded with a nod. "Your students adore you; even my kids are crazy about you, Nicholas."

He kissed her. "Thank you for being so understanding and supportive. A week ago, I didn't know I even had a daughter. Now I'm about to meet her..." Nicholas shook his head in disbelief. "I don't know what to say to Zoe."

She touched his cheek. "You'll find the right words, Babe. Just be your loveable self."

The doorbell sounded.

He looked nervous but tried to shake it off. "They're here."

Grinning, Sheila nodded. "Yes, they are... the door, babe."

Nicholas planted a quick kiss on her lips, then moved to open the front door.

Diana rushed into his arms, pulling him close to her and pressing her ample breasts against his chest.

He glanced over at Sheila while disengaging out of her embrace. "Hello Diana." Nicholas's gaze slid to the young woman standing beside his ex-wife.

"This is Zoe… your daughter."

She reached out to shake his hand. "It's nice to meet you."

Diana looked past him to where Sheila stood near the bottom of the staircase. Her smile disappeared. "Who is *she*?"

She's my girlfriend," he said. "Sheila Moore."

Folding her arms across her chest, Diana muttered, "I see…"

"Is there a problem?" Nicholas asked.

"I envisioned this moment just being about our daughter."

"Sheila's a very important part of my life so I asked her to be here." Nicholas gestured for her to come join them.

Diana planted a fake smile on her lips. "How nice to meet you."

"Same," Sheila murmured, then said, "Your daughter is gorgeous."

"She gets her looks from her mother."

"Mama…"

"Well, you do," Diana stated.

"She does look a lot like you," Sheila agreed.

"Why don't we go into the living room?" Nicholas suggested. Diana definitely wasn't at all thrilled about Sheila being there, but he didn't care. He'd promised Sheila they were a team, even in this situation. She had an uncanny ability to identify hidden agendas. Nicholas didn't trust Diana and neither did Sheila. He could see it in her gaze.

―――――――――

SHEILA FOLDED her slender arms across her breasts and shivered as cold air from the air-conditioning vents swirled around her. She glanced down at her navy slacks and navy and while cotton shell. She suddenly wished she'd worn something else—something more couture. Diana was draped in a beautiful dress with chic purse and shoes; all by the same designer. Sheila chided herself. This wasn't a competition. Nicholas's heart already belonged to her.

She shivered once more. It wasn't that the room was cold. This time it was from the memory of his kisses—kisses that ignited a flame of passion overtaking Sheila to the point she felt as if she couldn't take another breath. A reminder that she was the woman he desired. Nicholas had chosen her.

The tiny hairs on her body stood to attention. Sheila looked up to find Diana staring at her. She had no trouble meeting the woman's hard, assessing gaze. She lifted her chin in slight defiance and boldly stared back. Nicholas and Zoe were in conversation and didn't notice the silent exchange. Diana was attractive—Sheila couldn't take that from her. Her body was toned. She most likely exercised on a regular basis. Her mocha toned complexion was smooth and her make-up applied with a light hand.

This woman don't know me, Sheila thought, fighting a battle of personal restraint. *She has no idea what I'm capable of doing to her.* She didn't want to revert back to the *old* Sheila, but she was not one to play with.

Diana finally looked away and back at Nicholas. She remarked once more, "You know... I actually think Zoe looks just like you. She just doesn't have those beautiful gray eyes."

Sheila rolled her eyes heavenward. The woman was boldly flirting with him in her face.

No respect.

There was a time when Sheila used to do the same thing. Back then she had no idea just how pathetic and desperate she must have looked. *Thank you, Lord for giving me a desire to change my behavior for the better.*

"I'm sure you must be hungry," Nicholas said. "Why don't we grab some food?"

Sheila touched his arm. "You all go ahead. I promised Kiya and Gray we'd have dinner together. They're picking me up shortly."

He eyed her. "Are you sure about this?"

She nodded. "I think it should just be the three of you tonight. You and Zoe have a lot of catching up to do. Your daughter deserves your full attention." She wanted to show that she trusted Nicholas and his love for her.

He kissed her, then whispered, "This is one of the reasons I love you. I'll call you later."

Diana sent Sheila a sharp glare.

She responded with a smile. "Enjoy your dinner."

"Oh, we will."

Sheila was unbothered by Diana's response. She trusted Nicholas.

She'd texted Kiya to come pick her up a few minutes after meeting his ex-wife. Her daughter was outside.

Sheila got into the front seat on the passenger side.

"Mama, how did it go with Professor Washington and his daughter?" Kiya asked.

"It went well," she stated. "Zoe seems very sweet, but her mother... There's something about her that just doesn't ring true to me. She's up to something."

"Did you tell Professor Washington?"

Sheila shook her head no. "It's just a gut feeling, Kiya. I can't say anything to Nicholas without any evidence. He'll only assume that I'm jealous which I'm not."

"How do you feel about him having a daughter?" Gray asked from the backseat of the car.

"He's always wanted to be a father," Sheila responded. "I'm happy for him."

Fifteen minutes later, they were at the restaurant.

Once they were seated, the trio ordered drinks which arrived a few minutes later.

Kiya took a long sip of her soda, then inquired, "Do you really believe that she's really his child? Does Zoe look anything like him?"

"She resembles her mother actually."

"I just want to know if she's cute," Gray interjected.

Sheila and Kiya chuckled.

Their waitress came to take their orders.

When she walked away, Gray asked, "Why didn't you want to go to dinner with them?"

Settling back in the booth, Sheila responded, "Because I'd rather be here with the two of you instead of sitting there with Nicholas's ex-wife shooting daggers at me with her eyes."

"Mama, you don't like her," Kiya stated. "I can see it in the expression on your face."

Her daughter was right. Sheila didn't trust her one bit. "You should've seen the way she was all over Nicholas. Talk about thirsty…" Her feeling that Diana was up to something continued to intensify throughout the evening.

The fact that she didn't bother to have a paternity test done as soon as Zoe was born puzzled Sheila. According to Nicholas, he and Diana were still intimate during that time, so why did she just assume the child belonged to the man she was having an affair with and not her own husband? Sheila reasoned that it might be because Zoe didn't have gray eyes like Nicholas.

She hated that he had to wait so long to find out he'd fathered a child—something he's desperately wanted for years.Sheila once wanted to give him this desire of his heart, but the way MS affected her body—she made the decision to not have a child naturally. She never once regretted this choice. Sheila was grateful to have Kiya and Gray. She loved them more than she'd ever loved anyone else, including Nicholas. They were *her* children—nothing would ever change that.

"Professor Washington said his daughter and I are the

same age," Kiya stated. "I'm looking forward to meeting her."

"It's too bad she's in school up north somewhere." Sheila laid down her menu. "I'm sure Nicholas would love to have her attend the university."

Kiya took a sip of her drink. "How long will they be in town?"

"Just for the weekend, I'm assuming. Zoe has to get back for her classes."

Chapter 8

THIS WAS NOT the reunion she'd pictured in her mind.

Diana wasn't prepared to find Nicholas with a girlfriend. She shuttered inward at the thought of him with another woman.

He'd never once indicated he was seeing someone when they talked on the phone. She'd done her research and knew he wasn't married but could never find anything about a love interest.

She couldn't believe Nicholas would have her present for the moment he met his daughter for the first time. Apparently, Sheila meant a great deal to him, and this bothered Diana.

If this tramp thought she was gonna be Zoe's stepmother, then she had another thought coming. Diana didn't just come to Charleston to reunite Nicholas with his daughter—she hoped this reunion would lead to them getting back together.

Terrible regrets assailed her for walking out on him all those years ago. She was young and foolish. Now that she was older, she knew exactly what she wanted. But first she had to find a way to eliminate the competition.

"Mom..."

She glanced over at Zoe. "What is it, sugar?"

"You okay?"

Diana nodded. "I'm great. I can tell Nick already loves you."

"He doesn't really know me."

"It doesn't matter," she responded. "He's always wanted children. You're his only child."

"He's dating someone."

"She can barely stand up without that fancy looking cane," Diana uttered. "Do you really think Nick's gonna have children with her. She's got to be a good fifteen years older than him."

"Mama, you shouldn't talk about her disability like that," Zoe admonished. "And she doesn't look old to me. They're probably the same age."

"You're right," she agreed. "I shouldn't have said anything about her cane, but she's older than me and Nick for sure. I don't know why he felt she needed to be here. This should have just been about the three of us."

"Maybe they're really serious."

Diana chewed her bottom lip. "Or she just thinks they are. I didn't get that vibe from Nick."

"I did," Zoe responded.

"I'm sure she nagged him to let her be here. Did you see the way she watched me? I almost asked if she wanted to take a picture. I can tell that she's threatened by me."

"You really think so?"

Diana nodded. "I do. Hey, I'd be worried about me, too. I look great and I have the body of an athlete. She's skinny and frail looking."

"Mama, you play tennis four days a week and you love working out. I'm pretty sure Sheila has MS or some other disease."

"Like I said," Diana stated, "no competition at all."

"WHAT HOTEL ARE YOU STAYING AT?" Nicholas inquired while they waited for Zoe to exit the restroom. He'd already paid the check and intended to drop them off before heading home.

Diana glanced over her shoulder to see if Zoe was on her way back to the table. "I made reservations at a hotel, but...I just found out Steve canceled all my credit cards. I don't have a lot of cash, Nick...we don't have anywhere to stay. How could he do this to me and my daughter?" she questioned. "I had to withdraw Zoe from school because he said he wasn't going to pay for her education anymore. He's really being a jerk about all this." Her eyes watered.

Nicholas couldn't believe what he was hearing. "Maybe I should talk to him man to man..."

"You're the last person Steve wants to hear from right now," Diana uttered, then shrugged. "I don't know what to do, but I'll figure something out."

"You and Zoe are welcome to stay with me for the weekend," Nicholas said. "I have the space." He wasn't sure how Sheila would feel about this, but he couldn't leave them stranded. Besides it was only for the weekend.

Diana looked relieved. "How do you think your girlfriend will feel about this? I'm not here to cause problems for you."

"Feel about what?" Zoe interjected when she sat down at the table.

"I invited you and your mom to stay with me. As for Sheila—she'll will be fine with it." The truth was that she would be anything but okay with this arrangement, but Nicholas didn't feel he had a choice.

"Thank you, Nick," Diana said. "We really appreciate your offer." While he was busy paying the check, she winked at her daughter.

———

"MAKE YOURSELF COMFORTABLE," Nicholas said to them when they returned to the house. "Would you like some tea or a bottle of water?"

Diana looked all around her. She didn't get a chance to see much of it before they left for dinner. The house was beautiful and airy; wide-open with dove gray walls and comfortable furniture, but she could tell it was expensive. "Tea is fine, thank you."

Zoe walked over to her and said, "I'm afraid to touch anything. I don't want to accidentally break something that costs more than everything I own."

Diana agreed. She slowly made her way through the house, admiring the living room, stopping briefly to look at a couple of personal pictures on the fireplace mantle. She moved closer, scanning the group shots of his family.

She smiled when she glimpsed a photo of Jake and Tori Madison with their children.

"I know we just ate, but sometimes I get snacky. I have some chips and guacamole," Nicholas said. He set the platter out on the table with a pitcher of iced tea and three glasses.

Zoe descended on the chips and Diana busied herself pouring glasses of tea for all of them. Taking a sip, she looked over the railing at the ocean sprawled out ahead of them. It was a beautiful afternoon, warm but with a light breeze that kept it from being too hot. It was a perfect day to spend on the beach and she was glad that Nicholas had invited them to stay. They had a much better view here than they would have at the hotel.

Nicholas glanced at his daughter. "You good?"

Smiling, Zoe nodded.

"I'm having a great time," Diana interjected. "I haven't been this relaxed in ages."

"You really have a beautiful house," Zoe said. "Mama told me that you have another house in Georgia too."

"I do," he confirmed. "On St. Simon's Island. I'll be hosting Thanksgiving dinner there, so you'll get to see it."

"Great," she responded.

Diana avoided Nicholas's gaze. She knew he was probably wondering how she knew about his beach house. She should've told Zoe not to mention it to anyone.

Too late now.

Chapter 9

AFTER HE MADE sure they had everything they needed, he retired to his bedroom. Nicholas sat down in one of the chairs in the sitting area and called Sheila.

"Hey beautiful," Nicholas said, smiling when she answered.

"How was dinner?"

"Everything was good. I just wish you'd been there with us."

"I know, but I really think you and Zoe needed this time together without me."

"Diana and Zoe are going to be staying with me," Nicholas announced.

"I thought they had hotel reservations," she responded.

He could tell by her tone that she wasn't happy with this piece of news. "They did. Apparently, Diana's husband canceled her credit cards, and she doesn't carry a lot of cash.

Sweetheart, I couldn't leave them on the streets. Besides, I think having Zoe at the house will enable us to really get to know one another. It's only for the weekend."

"I understand your daughter staying with you, but Diana? Nicholas, are you sure about this? If it were me, I'd pay for her to stay in a hotel."

"Diana wants to be with Zoe. I can understand why she's being so protective," Nicholas stated.

"She's up to something," Sheila said. "I know women like her. I was one of them not too long ago."

"Diana's going through a really hard time."

"She's getting a divorce, Nicholas. People do it all the time. She'll survive."

"Are you jealous?" he asked.

"No, I'm not," Sheila responded. "I just don't trust your ex-wife. Something just doesn't ring true for me."

"Why do you say that?" Nicholas asked.

"It's a feeling I'm getting. Babe, just be careful around her."

"Are we still on for breakfast tomorrow?" he inquired.

"Sure. What about Zoe and her mother?"

"I'll be back here in time to take them to lunch and take them sightseeing."

"I'll see you in the morning then."

He grinned. "Yes, you will. Goodnight, sweetheart."

Nicholas was looking forward to having breakfast with Sheila and her kids. He would've loved to take Zoe with him, but felt it was too soon. He wanted to spend some time with

Sheila even if it was just breakfast. The rest of his weekend was devoted to Zoe and Diana.

———————

DIANA TOOK it upon herself to prepare a delicious breakfast for the three of them. She recalled how he used to love her cooking. *I'll give Nick a delicious reminder of what he's been missing.*

Nicholas entered the kitchen, his eyes traveling around at all the food on the counter. "What's all this?"

"I made all your favorites as a special thank you for letting us stay with you." She deliberately allowed her silk robe to fall open, revealing a sheer nightie beneath. Diana chuckled. "I guess I got a little carried away. I'm sure you remember how much I love to cook."

"I'm afraid I won't be able to join you. I've already made plans to have breakfast with Sheila."

"Surely she'd understand…"

Nicholas shook his head. "We made these plans a few days ago. Whatever's left… you can put it away for tomorrow."

"You're seriously gonna just leave after I've made all this food." Her tone was laced with anger and disappointment.

"Diana, don't you think you should've checked with me *before* you did all this?"

"I just assumed you'd be here for breakfast," she responded. "Especially since your daughter and I just got here."

"I'm sorry but Sheila and I had this breakfast planned before I knew you were coming. She graciously backed out of our plans for dinner last night. Diana, I need you to understand that she's very important to me—we're going to be spending a lot of time together."

"Is it serious between you?"

"Yes, it is," Nicholas confirmed. "Sheila's the woman I intend to marry."

Diana met his gaze. "I'm sorry for overstepping."

"Next time, just check with me first."

"Of course."

"I really don't know what he sees in that woman," Diana uttered when Nicholas left the house. "I'm not even sure she actually has multiple sclerosis. For all we know, Sheila could be using that cane and faking to gain Nick's sympathy."

"I think she's really got it," Zoe responded. "Besides my dad isn't stupid. He wouldn't even deal with her if that were the case."

———

"WHAT'S WRONG?" Sheila asked when Nicholas arrived the next morning.

"Diana got up this morning and cooked a spread. She got upset when I told her I had plans with you."

"I'm sure she didn't appreciate that piece of news."

Nicholas shrugged. "It's not my problem. I told her to check in with me in the future going forward."

"You do know she has an agenda. Diana wants you back."

"That's not going to happen. Our connection was severed years ago."

"I feel like she's using your daughter as a pawn," Sheila stated.

"I'm hope she knows better than to do something like that."

"From where I'm standing, it doesn't mean she does, or she simply doesn't care."

Nicholas embraced her. "I'm where I want to be."

"I appreciate it, babe. But you need to spend time with Zoe. I'm not going anywhere."

"I have the rest of the day with her," Nicholas said. "We had this date a couple of weeks ago and I didn't want to cancel on you or Gray. He asked me to be the stand-in for his father and I told him I would—I'm not backing out." The football team was hosting a breakfast for the mothers. All the fathers were asked to help with the cooking and serving.

"I know Gray appreciates it," Sheila said. Placing her hand to his cheek, she added, "You're so sweet for doing this."

"He's a part of my family."

His words brought tears of joy to her eyes. Sheila blinked rapidly to keep them from falling. She felt like the luckiest woman alive.

Chapter 10

"I'M GOING to see an old friend," Diana announced after she cleaned the kitchen. "I'll be back in an hour." She needed details on Sheila Moore, and she knew exactly where to go to get the information.

Tori Madison.

Her husband Jake was Sheila's business partner. Diana was sure Tori would have details on the woman Nick proclaimed he wanted to marry.

She'd gotten the information off the website and drove to the bookstore. Diana wasn't sure how she was going to be received since she'd met Tori through Nicholas. She was sure he'd told Tori about the way Diana left their marriage.

She sat in the car, summoning up the courage to go inside the shop. Diana had been in the parking lot for the past ten minutes. She inhaled deeply, then exhaled slowly.

Diana got out the vehicle and strode with purpose toward the entrance.

When she walked inside, she spotted Tori talking to a customer.

They made eye contact and Diana glimpsed the moment recognition dawned in Tori's gaze.

"Diana... oh my goodness," she exclaimed, rushing toward her. "It's been a while..."

"Yes, it has," she responded.

"What brings you to Charleston?"

"It's time for Nick to meet his daughter," she blurted, going straight to the point. "I thought I was carrying another man's child."

"*Nicholas is a father*," Tori uttered in shock. "Oh, I know he's completely over the moon. He's wanted a child for so long."

"Yeah... I just hated we found out eighteen years later."

"Did Nicholas know about the affair?"

"He didn't," Diana responded. "He's still trying to process everything."

"I can imagine," Tori murmured.

"When we arrived yesterday, Nick wasn't alone," she stated. "He's seeing Sheila Moore. I know that she and Jake are business partners. I need you to tell me everything about her, especially if she's gonna be around my daughter. Is she a good person?"

"She and I have had some major issues in the past, but she seems to have changed. We don't talk on the regular. If and when I see her, we're cordial."

"What happened?" Diana inquired.

"There's no need to go into it now," Tori said. "We settled it years ago—I don't want to rehash it."

"I'm happy to see that you and Jake are still together. I thought Steve and I would be together forever, but I must confess that the stress of living with a total stranger who may be the worst thing that happened to you—I don't feel it anymore. Steve and I weren't meant to be."

"Have you two tried marriage counseling?" Tori asked.

"He wasn't interested," Diana responded. "Trust me, I tried to convince him. Then finding out that Zoe wasn't his daughter... that was the fatal blow to our marriage." She feigned like she was wiping tears from her eyes.

Tori gave her a sympathetic look. "I'm so sorry."

Diana smiled. "I'm not. Nick is a good man and I want Zoe to get to know her real father."

"I need to check on my customer. I'll be back."

"I can't believe my eyes..." Charlene stopped short when she walked out of the stock room. "Diana Washington..."

"Hey Charlene... it's now Diana Winston."

"What are you doing here in Charleston?"

"I came to introduce Nick to his daughter Zoe."

A soft gasp escaped Charlene. "Excuse me?"

"It's a long story. But yes... he and I have a daughter."

"Oh wow. That's wonderful."

"We had a lovely meeting," Diana stated. "The only thing I didn't like was that he had his girlfriend there. *Sheila Moore.*"

Charlene rolled her eyes heavenward. "Yep... he's seeing

her. Personally, I think he could do so much better, but it's not my business."

"Tori mentioned the two of them had issues at one time."

"Cheating is more than a just an issue," Charlene uttered in a low voice.

"Jake had an affair with Sheila?" Diana asked.

"Yep."

"I knew she couldn't be trusted. Does Nick know about all this."

"He does."

"And he's okay with it?" Diana shook her head. "I can't believe this."

"He really cares for her. According to Nicholas, she's not that same person she was back then."

"I'm not so sure."

"Diana, why are you so concerned with Sheila?" Charlene asked. "Are you trying to reunite with Nicholas?"

"What if I am?" Diana questioned.

"I don't think it's a good idea," Tori uttered when she joined them. "You broke his heart when you walked away from your marriage. It took him a while to get over it. I thought you wanted to work on your marriage, Diana."

"It takes two people to make a marriage work and Steve isn't willing."

"To be honest, it doesn't really sound as if you're willing either." Tori glanced over at Charlene who nodded in agreement.

"Only because of the way he treated my daughter. He's

cut us off financially, including her college tuition. I had to withdraw her from school."

"That's terrible," Tori murmured.

"I don't care if he hurts me, but my child..." Diana shook her head. "You don't mess with my baby."

Charlene and Tori nodded in agreement.

"So where are you staying?" Tori asked.

"With Nicholas."

Charlene glanced at her cousin, then back at Diana. "Really?"

"Yeah. He wanted us to stay in the house with him—said he'd have it no other way. In fact, we're going to church tomorrow as a family."

"Sounds like you and Nicholas are getting along pretty well," Charlene said as she walked around the huge display counter.

"It's almost like we're not divorced. We're keeping it very civil for Zoe. She's been through enough with her stepfather."

"I'm not surprised," Tori said. "Nicholas doesn't do drama except in his books."

"Well, I'd better get back to my daughter. It's great seeing you again."

Tori smiled. "You, too. I look forward to meeting your daughter."

"I'll bring her by the shop one day next week. She loves to read." Diana headed to the door, releasing a soft sigh of relief.

Her instincts were on point where Sheila was concerned. The woman was nothing more than a home-wrecker. "You don't deserve an ounce of happiness for what you've done,"

Diana whispered as she got into the car and headed back to the townhouse.

EARLY SUNDAY MORNING, the phone rang while Nicholas was getting dressed to attend church services.

It was Sheila.

"I know you're about to leave for church, but I just got off the phone with my mother's friend, Minnie. She said my mom's not feeling well and is refusing to go to the hospital. I'm going to Frogmore. This sounds bad, Nicholas."

"You're in no condition to drive. I'll take you there."

"I can have Gray drive me."

"No, I'll take you, Sheila. No need to worry the kids until you find out what's going on with your mother."

"I appreciate it. My nerves are on edge."

"I'll be there shortly, sweetheart."

"Thank you."

Nicholas found Diana downstairs drinking a cup of coffee. She was dressed in a navy dress and matching pumps.

"Good morning. Zoe should be down in a few minutes. She went back upstairs to get her purse."

"Good morning," he greeted. "I know we had plans to attend church, but you and Zoe will have to go without me. Sheila's mom is sick, so I'm taking her to Frogmore."

"I hope her mother gets well soon."

"I don't know how long we'll be gone."

"Don't worry. I won't be cooking. Zoe and I planned to

have lunch somewhere after church and then do some exploring. We can take care of ourselves."

"I'll call you when we get there."

"Uh huh…" Diana uttered.

"Do you have a problem?" Nicholas asked.

"Actually, I do," Diana stated. "Your daughter comes to town to get to know you and suddenly Sheila needs your attention every day. I know she's your girlfriend, but I would think you'd like to get to know Zoe."

"This is an emergency and I'm not about to neglect her. Sheila's not able to drive right now, so that's why I'm taking her to see her mom."

"She's got kids, right? I'm sure they have driver licenses."

"Sheila and I don't want them to know anything about her mother's condition just yet. Surely you can understand our reasoning."

Diana gave a reluctant nod.

"By the way, what time is your flight leaving?" Nicholas inquired.

"We're not leaving tomorrow."

He stopped in his tracks. "Oh?"

"Nick let's just talk when you get back. Since Sheila needs you right now, you should go."

He didn't like Diana's attitude, but wanted to keep it peaceful for Zoe. She'd already had to deal with a lot of drama between her mom and stepdad. Zoe had enough to process.

"WHERE'S NICHOLAS?" Zoe asked, looking around.

"Sheila had a family emergency, so he had to take off to be by her side," Diana uttered. "He said her mother is sick."

"You think she's making it up?"

"I don't know, but I wouldn't put it past that woman."

"We might as well leave then. He says his pastor is really good." Zoe headed to the door.

"I'm not in the mood. I can't believe Nick."

"Mama, it's okay. Sheila could be telling the truth about her mom. He should be by her side."

"He should be here for you, Zoe. You're going through a lot right now as well. Nick should be putting you first."

Her phone vibrated.

Zoe glanced down to read the message. "It's from Nicholas. He apologized and said we will talk when he gets back."

"That's not good enough," Diana uttered.

"Let's just go to church. Maybe you'll feel better after."

"I doubt it."

"Mama, you can't just expect Nicholas to suddenly do everything right. He didn't know I existed until a week ago. You have to give him a break."

"And you shouldn't let him off the hook so easily, Zoe. Sugar, I know what I'm doing. I just need you to trust me and do what I tell you to do. You do that and we will soon be a family again."

Chapter 11

NICHOLAS DROVE ALONG ROUTE 21. Sheila had seen her mother two weeks ago and noticed then that Essie Moore didn't look well. She'd even advised Essie to call her doctor and schedule a doctor's appointment.

"She hates doctors... I think she's mostly afraid," Sheila mumbled. "I'm not crazy about them myself."

"How was she the last time you saw her?" he asked.

"Ma said she was fine, but she didn't look it to me." Sheila wasn't looking forward to the conversation, but she was taking her mother to see a doctor. She's arranged to get her in today at noon.

Staring out the window, Sheila recalled how much she once hated Frogmore. There was a time she wanted nothing to do with this place.

As they neared her childhood home, Sheila mentally prepared herself for what was sure to be a confrontation.

Essie lived in the house at the end of the street.

Nicholas parked in front of a wooden shanty that sat up on short columns of brick and cinderblock in a dirt yard. He got out, walked around to the passenger side and opened the door for her.

She stepped out of the vehicle. Taking in her surroundings, Sheila stood in place, using her cane for support.

She eyed the old house which was desperately in need of repair. "If she's going to continue to live here—Ma's going to have to let me get this place renovated. I'm going to have to have it torn down and built from scratch." The mere sight of splintered and rotting wood around the doorjambs and windows made her skin crawl. Growing up, she could hear the rats crawling around in the walls. Her mother still kept haint blue paint around the doorway and windows to keep the evil spirits away, but it did nothing for the critters that often entered through some discovered opening in the roof from time to time.

A stocky woman walked out of the house. "Come chile... come'yah... come see yo mammy."

"Miss Minnie, how is she doing?"

"She not doin' too good."

Sheila took Nicholas's hand and made her way up the steps to the porch.

Her mother was in her bedroom.

He gestured to the sofa and said, "I'll wait out here for you."

Sheila knocked, then opened the door. "Ma..."

"Uh thought Uh heard yo voice. W'y you don' call me tuh say you comin'?"

"Miss Minnie told me that you're not feeling well. I made a doctor's appointment for you."

"Uh no need doctor," Essie uttered.

Sheila gave her mother a kiss on the cheek before taking a seat on the sofa. "Ma, you're sick." She was a tiny woman, but now she looked frailer than before.

"Uh have tuh cancer. Nuthin' you can do."

"*Cancer*... Ma... why didn't you tell me?" Her eyes teared up.

"Uh been tinkin' 'bout you."

"I'm doing fine, Ma. What are the doctors saying?" Sheila asked.

"H-Hospice..."

Essie surveyed Sheila's face. Shaking her head, she uttered, "Nooo... uh be wit tuh Lawd soon. Don't be sad."

"Ma, I need you. You can't leave me." Tears stung the backs of Sheila's eyes. "The kids and I need you." She reached over and took her mother's hand in her own. "I'll arrange to have an ambulance bring you to my house. I'll take care of you."

Essie nodded. "That be fine."

It bothered Sheila that her mother didn't put up a fight.

This was bad.

Really bad.

Essie closed her eyes.

"She just sleeping," Minnie said from the doorway.

"Why didn't you tell me about my mother?" Sheila asked. "I could've gotten her the best doctors…"

"She no wan tuh worry you, chile."

Sheila sighed in resignation. "I need her doctor's information. I'm going to have her moved to my house."

Minnie nodded in agreement.

"What type of cancer?"

"Pancreatic."

Sheila stared out the window. "I'm sorry but death is not an option."

"Yo' mama say she not afraid to die. She made her peace with Gawd."

"I'm not giving up on her," Sheila stated. "I'm going to find the best doctors to help rid her body of cancer." Tears streaming down her face, she glanced over at her mother, then to where Minnie stood. "I'm not ready to lose her."

The older woman embraced her.

Sheila left the bedroom and joined Nicholas in the living room. "Ma has pancreatic cancer. I need to make arrangements to transport her to my house. I'm not leaving her here."

"I'll make the preparations," he responded. "You go back to your mother."

He hugged her.

"Pray for my mama, Nicholas," Sheila whispered. "Please pray for her healing."

Nicholas kissed her cheek. "It's done."

He looked up the number for an ambulance company and made a quick call.

Sheila went back to her mother's room. She knew that Nicholas would take care of everything—it was one less thing she had to worry about."

Four hours later, Sheila released a soft sigh when the ambulance pulled into her driveway. The drive had exhausted her, and she was glad to be home.

The circular flower bed filled with roses in vibrant colors lined the edge of the path to the porch. She glanced up at the crepe myrtles standing guard on both sides of the house.

The ambulance backed into the driveway and parked.

Sheila unlocked the door, and Nicholas held it open for the paramedics to bring in her mother.

"You can put her in this room," she told them. Sheila made a mental note to purchase a hospital bed.

Gray walked out of the kitchen eating a sandwich. "What's wrong with Grandma?"

"She's going to be staying with us for a while. Mama's sick."

"How sick?"

"She has cancer."

"Your mom's calling for you," Nicholas said.

Sheila gave him a grateful smile. "I'll be right back."

"How are you holding up?" Nicholas asked.

"I don't really know," Sheila responded. "I'm just in shock. I don't understand why Mama wouldn't tell me she had cancer."

"I'm sure Miss Essie didn't want to worry you and the kids."

"I'm scared, Nicholas," Sheila confessed. She'd never been

one to show vulnerability, but since her diagnosis, her life had changed in so many ways.

"Is everything okay," Diana asked when Nicholas arrived home later in the day.

"No. Miss Essie has cancer. Sheila took her home with her."

"Oh wow... she didn't know?"

"Her mother didn't tell her."

Diana felt a twinge of guilt over the way she'd acted earlier. She honestly felt Sheila was trying to manipulate Nick to keep him away from Zoe. Apparently, she'd been wrong. However, Diana still didn't care for her.

"Where's Zoe?"

"She's upstairs in her room."

Nicholas went up to talk to her.

His abrupt escape, leaving her alone in the living room. Diana noticed that he never seemed to hang around her long. The only time he tolerated her presence was when Zoe was with them.

He still has feelings for me. A smile tumbled from her lips. Diana walked over to a photograph of him, picking it up. "I know you still love me. I can feel it," she whispered.

Almost two hours later, Nicholas descended the stairs alone. "Nick, we need to talk," Diana said.

"About what?"

"You should know that Zoe and I don't have a place to

live. I can't afford a place of my own right now. I'm gonna have to take Steve to court. I don't know how long all that will take."

Nicholas was speechless.

"Do you mind if we stay here until I can get some things worked out? Hopefully, it'll only be a week or two—three weeks at the most."

"Steve can't just put you and Zoe out like that. The two of you have been married for a long time. You're also the mother of his children. Legally—"

"I don't want to stay anywhere I'm not wanted," Diana interjected. "Zoe doesn't need to be in the middle of my drama. She has bouts of anxiety, Nick. She also suffers from depression. She didn't want you to know, so please don't mention it."

Sheila wasn't going to be thrilled about this turn of events at all. But now wasn't the time to discuss this with her.

"I'm not going to put you and Zoe on the street. You're welcome to stay here but understand that Sheila's going to be around."

"It's not a problem for me," Diana stated.

"What were you and my dad discussing?" Zoe asked when her mother came upstairs. "It looked pretty serious."

"He was telling me about Sheila's mom. The poor lady has cancer. We also discussed our staying here for a few weeks. This will give me some time to try and see what Steve is planning to do."

"You didn't go asking him for money, did you?"

"No, I didn't."

Diana wasn't thrilled about Sheila's situation, but was determined to use this time to draw Nicholas back into her life. She'd clearly bet on the wrong horse when it came to marriage, but fate had provided an opportunity to correct her mistake. Diana intended to do just that.

Chapter 12

SHEILA WAS A WOMAN ON A MISSION.

Nicholas admired the way she took on caring for her mother. Between her and Valerie, Essie was in good hands. However, her condition continued to worsen. Although he had no idea how much time the doctor had given Essie, Nicholas suspected that it wasn't long. On his most recent visit, he noticed that she'd lost more weight, had little to no appetite and was growing progressively weaker.

Nicholas continued to hold onto hope and pray fervently for the Lord to heal Essie. He refused to stop believing in miracles—they happened every day. "Please don't take Miss Essie," he whispered. "She loves you and is a good woman. Her daughter and grandchildren still need her. Please save her. I want her to bear witness to my marriage to her daughter. I want to dance with her at my wedding... Lord, if it be your will, please heal her on this side. If not, give her family the strength to accept that you've received her home. Amen."

He heard a noise behind him and turned to find Zoe in the doorway. Nicholas pasted on a smile. "Hey you..."

"How are you doing?" she inquired.

"I'm good."

"How is Sheila?"

"She's hanging in there. She called me earlier to say that the doctor wanted to place her mom in a hospice facility, but Miss Essie wants to stay home."

"This has to be so hard on her."

He nodded. "Very hard. She's trying to be strong for Kiya and Gray. They adore their grandmother."

Diana strolled into the room where they were talking. "I was thinking we could take Zoe sightseeing and maybe grab some lunch... we could have a picnic at the waterfront."

"Mama... I don't think this is the time..." Zoe said.

"I think it's the perfect time," she countered. "Nicholas, you need a break to just relax and have fun for a few hours."

He felt bad for not spending much time with his daughter. She was sweet and understanding, but Nicholas wanted to be fair to both Zoe and Sheila. Diana was the only one who complained about how much time he spent away from the house. She acted more like a wife than an ex and he didn't like it one bit.

The timing was terrible, but Nicholas wasn't going to abandon Sheila and her children when they needed him the most. He also wasn't going to ignore Zoe either. They always had breakfast together and ended the evening with a movie, dessert or just talking.

"Nick…" Diana prompted. "What do you say?"

"I promised Sheila I'd go to the funeral home with her," he responded. "She wants my help to pick out a coffin."

"Oh my… I didn't know things were that bad."

"Unfortunately, it's not looking good at all," Nicholas stated.

"Please give Sheila our condolences."

"Mama, the lady isn't dead yet," Zoe interjected.

"Nick, you know what I meant."

He nodded.

Rising to his feet, Nicholas said, "I'd better get going. Zoe, I'll see you later tonight. Pick out something good to watch."

She smiled. "I will."

"Did you see the way he just ignored me?" Diana asked her daughter, her expression clouded in anger.

"I don't think he meant nothing by it. Nicholas has a lot on his mind right now."

Diana's mood veered sharply to anger. "He never spends any time with me—he barely even talks to me unless it's necessary. I've got enough stress dealing with Steve. I don't need Nick angry with me, too."

"Mama, he's nice to you."

"There are things we still need to discuss."

"Like what?"

"I need to make Nick understand what happened back then. I want to apologize but he won't give me a chance. I just need to talk to him alone."

"Maybe he's not ready for that, Mama. You basically sprung me on the man—Nicholas didn't know anything about me. Did you really expect him to just welcome us with open arms?"

"I don't know what I expected," Diana responded. "I guess I hoped it would be like old times between us."

"Maybe he needs more time to get used to the idea of having a daughter."

"You might be right, Zoe. Regardless, we're not going anywhere. Nick's not gonna be able to get rid of us.

ESSIE MOORE PASSED AWAY PEACEFULLY at 10 p.m. surrounded by her daughter, grandchildren, and Nicholas. Sheila was reading her favorite book in the Bible as she slipped away into a final sleep.

Nicholas would've preferred to stay with Sheila, but she sent him home. She was trying to be strong for her children. He wanted to be her strength.

When he arrived home, Diana and Zoe was nowhere in sight. Nicholas had called them from the car to tell them about Essie's death.

He went upstairs to his bedroom.

Nicholas opened the door and stopped dead in his tracks. "Diana, what are you doing in my room?" His ex-wife sat in the middle of his bed without a stitch of clothing on her body.

"I figured you might be in some need of comfort," she responded seductively. "I know you've been taking care of Sheila and her kids, but who's taking care of you?"

Averting his eyes, Nicholas said, "I need you to get dressed and get out of my room."

"We had a great sex life, Nick. I know you haven't forgotten how good we were together."

"If it was so great, why did you feel the need to step outside our marriage, Diana?"

"I deserve that," she murmured. "Nick, I can't change the past. I wish I could, but I can't. I'm sorry for what I did and all I want is a second chance with you."

"Diana, that's not going to happen. We are over."

"How is it you're so willing to be with a woman who tried to break up a marriage?"

"Are you serious right now?" Nicholas asked. "Diana, I'll give you ten minutes. When I come back up here—I want you out of my bedroom."

"When was the last time you made love to a real woman?" she challenged.

"I'm celibate."

Diana looked shocked. "You're *what*?"

"You heard me."

Nick and Sheila weren't sleeping together. This piece of information thrilled Diana. "You and I—we were married once."

"It doesn't matter. We're divorced now."

"Can you look me in the eye and tell me that you don't want me?" she asked.

Nicholas met her gaze. "I am not in the mood for this, Diana. I love Sheila and she's the only woman I want. Don't embarrass yourself any further. Get dressed and go to your room."

"I don't believe you."

"Go to your room, Diana."

Bewildered, he sat on the edge of his now empty bed. How could she even think that he'd want to bed her after everything that's happened. Not just with Sheila but the way she abandoned their marriage. She broke his heart and his trust a long time ago.

Chapter 13

THE STARK LIGHT of morning sunshine streaming through the bedroom window pulled Sheila from a fitful night of sleep and into the glare of harsh reality.

Her mother was gone.

Sheila sat up in bed, thinking back over the past two weeks.

She witnessed her mother's rapid decline as death drew closer. Hallucinations of family members long gone, murmurings and conversations that didn't make sense to Sheila—the doctor explained this was normal and one of the stages of active dying.

Tears welled up in her eyes.

My mother is dead. I'll never hear her voice again. I can never come to her for advice or just to talk.

Essie's last few days had been filled with persistent pain.

The doctor prescribed a morphine drip which provided some comfort enough for her to sleep.

A soft knock on the door cut into her thoughts.

Sheila wiped her face with the back of her hands. "Come in."

Kiya entered her bedroom with a tray of food. "I brought you something to eat. Professor Washington made breakfast."

She gave a slight nod. "How are you holding up, sweetie?"

"I'm numb."

"Where's Gray?" Sheila asked.

"Downstairs with Professor Washington."

"You know it's okay to call him Nicholas when you're not at school."

"I know, but it's less confusing this way for me."

"I went to the funeral home yesterday to pick out a coffin," Sheila stated. "I keep wondering if I hadn't done that —would she still be here with us."

Kiya sat down on the edge of the king-sized bed. "Mama, this was God's decision to take Grandma home. Even if you'd waited, we'd be in this same space. Grandma told me she was tired. She wanted to be with the Lord. She didn't like being in so much pain."

"I talked to the top oncologists in the world. I did everything I could to try to help her."

"I know that Mama."

"But it wasn't enough. She's gone and Ma's never coming back." Sheila wiped away her tears. "I'm being selfish, I know. I would rather have her here with me. I didn't want her to spend the rest of her days in pain. I wanted her healthy."

"Mama, she's healthy now—that's the way we have to think of this," Kiya said. "That's how I think of my mom— she's free from all the stuff she had to deal with in life. No more black eyes or broken arms. Gray and I don't have to hide in our closets anymore. Maybe my mom shouldn't have killed my dad, but when she shot him and then herself—she freed all of us."

"I'm so sorry you and Gray had to suffer through domestic violence. My father was verbally abusive toward my mom—it was horrible to listen to the things he'd call her. Back then I blamed my mom—I didn't know better. She endured a lot just to keep her family together. In the end, he walked out on us. Now that I'm older—it was the best thing he could've done for us. Once my mom got herself together— she was even a much better mother."

AFTER NICHOLAS CLEANED THE KITCHEN, he found Sheila outside sitting on the patio alone. He hadn't heard her come downstairs.

Nicholas was relieved when Kiya bought the empty plate back.

"You're sure you and Gray don't want to eat something?" He asked.

"I don't have an appetite right now," she responded. "Gray says he's not hungry either."

When Nicholas finished the dishes, he navigated outside and planted a kiss on Sheila's cheek. "Did you get any sleep last night?"

"Not really. I was up late working on funeral arrangements for Ma. I quit after three attempts to write her obituary. The words just wouldn't come. I think I'll have Kiya do it." Sheila took a long sip of her herbal tea. "Oh, how did everything go before Diana and her daughter left?"

"They haven't left yet," he answered. "You've been dealing with a lot, so I didn't want to bother you."

She placed her cup on the table. "I thought Zoe and her mother would be gone by now. You told me they were only staying for the weekend."

He heard the exasperation in her voice. "Sweetheart, you just lost your mother. We can discuss this later."

Sheila glanced at him. "What do we need to discuss?"

"We'll talk about it after the service," Nicholas stated.

"Diana asked if they could stay longer, right?"

He gave a slight nod. "They don't have anywhere else to go."

"She can go to her family in Brunswick," Sheila responded, her tone sharp and firm. "If not there, then I'm sure she must have a friend or two that will welcome them into their homes."

"Honey, let's table this until after the funeral."

"I knew she was going to pull something like this. That woman is thirsty." Sheila glanced over at him. "Has she already tried to seduce you?"

Nicholas chuckled.

"I'm not laughing. You need to get that woman out of your house."

"Sweetheart, I'm not some horny teenager. I can deal with Diana. Right now, I'm more concerned about you. How are you feeling?"

"I'm fine."

"Sheila, I know you. You're in a lot of pain right now, physically and emotionally. Don't push me away."

"Nicholas, you don't have to worry about me. Just check on the kids please. They're not saying much. They tend to internalize their feelings."

"They didn't eat anything for breakfast," Nicholas said. "I'll see if they're hungry now—they can go with me to pick up some food. Oh, I hope you don't mind. I told Tori about your mother's passing."

"I wondered how Jake found out. They sent over a huge bouquet of white roses from the staff. They came yesterday. Today another bouquet arrived from the New York office." A lone tear ran down her cheek. "I think a graveside service is appropriate since Ma didn't really attend a church."

"That sounds nice," Nicholas told her. "Is there anything I can do for you, sweetheart?"

"I just need you by my side," Sheila whispered. "I think this is probably the hardest thing I've ever had to do."

More tears flowed.

"I didn't always treat her right. I was even ashamed of her, but... if I had the chance to see her smile, hear her talk... it would be enough. I'd want to hug her one more time."

Nicholas moved his chair closer. "Your mother knew how much you loved her."

"I hope so."

"She did," Nicholas reassured her.

———

It rained hard Saturday afternoon for Essie's homegoing service. The day was dull and dreary, matching Sheila's mood as she eyed her reflection in the mirror, blinking back tears.

She chose a chic black and white color blocked dress with matching coat and a wide brim black and white hat. Her purse and matching shoes were black with a white trim.

A knock on her bedroom door drew Sheila out of her reverie.

"Come in."

Gray opened the door and entered. "I came to check on you. The people from the funeral home just got here."

"I'm okay," she responded softly. "I'll be out shortly." She tried to give him a brave smile but failed.

"Mama, I know that you're not okay," he responded. "None of us are doing well with this. I dreaded walking into that funeral home and seeing Grandma lying in that coffin last night. I don't know how I'm gonna do at the cemetery."

She walked over to her son and embraced him. "Me, too."

"I miss her already." Gray's eyes filled with tears and overflowed.

"My sweet son..." Sheila murmured. "We will see her

again. This is not a goodbye. We have to think of it more as a *see you later.*"

"Our family is never going to be the same," he said.

"No, but we will get through this. I hated seeing Ma waste away like that. I'm going to miss her, but I'm glad she's not in pain. This is the only thing that gives me a measure of comfort about my mother's death. She's free from sickness and worry."

"I know that you're right, but it doesn't make me feel any better."

Kiya stuck her head inside the doorway. "The limo is here."

Gray buttoned up his suit jacket and escorted Sheila out of the room.

They joined Minnie and a few of Essie's other friends' downstairs in the living room.

Nicholas arrived a few minutes later. Sheila wanted him to accompany her to the cemetery.

The funeral director escorted Sheila and the kids out first, holding a large black umbrella over their heads.

They were soon on their way.

Sheila stared out of the window, although nothing really captured her interest. Images of her and Essie formed in her mind. Despite some rough years when she and her mother were able to reconcile their relationship. They spent the past ten years laughing one moment, arguing the next, but there was always love between them. An unconscious smile formed on his lips.

Nicholas reached over and took her hand in his, giving it a gentle squeeze.

She glanced over at him and smiled.

The site where her mother would be buried was already surrounded by floral arrangements sent from all over the country. Essie's coffin was solid wood with rose gold column corners and swing bar handles. Her mother was not one for glitz, but Sheila was sure Essie would approve of the tasteful and elegant design.

She had no idea that Jake and Tori Madison were at the service until it was over.

Jake spoke for them both. "Sheila, I'm so sorry for your loss."

She cleared her throat softly. "Thank you both for coming. My mother had great respect for you, Jake. She would be thrilled to know that you came to her homegoing service. Tori, you're looking beautiful. Thank you for being here."

Sheila looked to Nicholas. "Please take me to the limo," she said in a low voice. "I need to get out of here."

Halfway to the car, Sheila felt her body weaken. She gripped the cane in her hand, then paused in her steps.

Nicholas embraced her. "I have you, sweetheart. If I have to pick you up and carry you—I will."

"I just needed a moment. I'm fine now." Sheila allowed her tears to run free the rest of the way. The thought of never hearing her mother's voice or seeing Essie again ripped through her heart.

She'd wiped away her tears and composed herself by the time Kiya and Gray came to the car.

Chapter 14

DIANA LOOKED out the window at the rain running down the pane. For a moment she paused, watching as lightning forked across the sky. They were pretty much stuck in the house while Nicholas was with Sheila.

She didn't know what it felt like to lose a parent, but she knew losing one was never easy. Still, it wasn't fair for Nicholas to just abandon them. Diana felt bad for Sheila, but death was a part of living. It would happen to each of them at some point.

With a sigh, she left the window to change into a pair of navy leggings and a snug, white tee-shirt. Diana gathered her hair into a careless ponytail. She expected Nicholas to arrive at any moment. He'd told Zoe he would be home after the service.

Diana kept checking the clock. What was taking him so long? She strolled over to the mirror and admired her reflection. She'd worked long and hard to keep her body in shape. Nicholas couldn't help but notice—she flaunted herself around him daily in tight-fitting clothes and workout gear, but he just averted his eyes and went on about his business, but she was going to force him to notice her.

SHEILA TOOK some medication the doctor prescribed for her to help her sleep once they were back at the house. Nicholas decided to take Kiya and Gray over to meet Zoe.

Diana entered the foyer just as he arrived. He could see the shock on her face at seeing his guests. Nicholas made the introductions.

"It's nice to meet you both," she managed. "My sincere condolences to your family on the loss of your grandmother."

"Thank you," they replied in unison.

"Where's Sheila?"

"At home resting," Nicholas responded. "Where's Zoe?"

"She's upstairs. I'll go get her."

"She didn't seem so happy to see us," Gray whispered when Diana left the room.

Kiya agreed.

"This is my house, and you're always welcome here," Nicholas stated.

Zoe descended the stairs.

"Hello," she said with a sincere smile. "Sheila must be your mother."

"Zoe, this is Kiya. She attends the university where I work and her brother Gray."

"Nice to meet you both," his daughter responded.

"I thought I'd take the three of you out for dinner and a movie." He looked at Kiya and Gray, then added, "If you're feeling up to it."

"Honestly, I need the distraction," Kiya said.

Her brother nodded in agreement.

"I don't mind cooking something," Diana offered from the bottom of the stairs.

"We'd rather go out," Zoe responded. "I'm in the mood for a good burger."

"Then you'll want to try Mr. Willie's burgers over by the school," Kiya responded. "They're the best in Charleston."

"They sure are," Nicholas and Gray said in unison.

They all burst into a round of laughter.

Nicholas's gaze traveled to where Diana was standing. He could tell she wasn't at all happy about not being included. He wanted to surround himself with his children. It's the way he thought of each one of them.

He knew Diana would have a few words for him when he returned, but Nicholas didn't care. She was a guest in his house and if she became a problem—they would have to find another solution for her.

DIANA WAS WAITING for Zoe in her room when she returned. "I thought you'd gone to bed already."

"What did you think of Kiya Moore?" she asked.

With a slight shrug, Zoe responded, "She seems nice enough. I like her."

"Oh noo…. don't you go thinking y'all gonna be friends—I don't want you hanging around Sheila's daughter. She might've inherited her mother's bad habits."

"I can't believe you," Zoe uttered. "What do you know about Sheila?"

"I know she tried to ruin Tori's marriage."

"Mom, you left my dad for another man, or did you forget about that?"

Diana sent her a sharp glare. "I won't have my mistakes thrown in my face by my own child. I've done too much for you."

"I'm just saying that everybody makes mistakes, Mama. It doesn't make her a bad person. And you can't blame Kiya for her mother's decisions."

"I'm simply looking out for you. They're outsiders. You and I are Nicholas's family. Eventually, he's gon' come around to seeing this. He may believe he wants Sheila, but what he really wants is his own family. *You and me.*"

"I'm not so sure…"

"Zoe, I know your father. Trust me on this. I'm going to get Nick back."

"Mom…"

"Can you support me for once please?" Diana questioned. "Nick and I have history. We've both grown up over the years—this time around we'll make it work."

"He has a girlfriend."

Shrugging in nonchalance, Diana said, "Doesn't matter." As far as she was concerned, Sheila didn't deserve to be in Nicholas's life.

I'm going to make her regret the day she ever met me.

Sheila had been nothing but a headache to Diana. Once the witch was out of Nicholas's life, he would finally welcome her home.

Diana spent the rest of the night thinking about revenge. It fueled and motivated her. Her ex-husband had reached out twice in the past two hours, but she had yet to respond to him. She was no longer interested in being his wife. She'd believed in him once and left the man she loved, choosing financial security. Now that Steve wasn't able to deliver on his promises, there was no point to their marriage.

Chapter 15

THE LAST WEEK of September was thrust upon Sheila. Her mother had been buried for two weeks now. With Essie gone, she was trying to decide what to do with her childhood home as well as a rental with a tenant moving out at the end of the month.

An hour later, Minnie called Sheila and asked if she'd be willing to rent the house to her niece who was getting married in a month.

"That won't be a problem as long as she pays the rent on time."

"She will."

Hanging up the phone, Sheila settled back against the cushions of her chair, hands to her face. Tears escaped her eyes, running down her face.

Ma... I didn't want you to leave me. I miss you so much already.

A loud knock cut into her grief.

Sheila composed herself, then went to answer the door.

A woman stood on the porch with a huge bouquet of yellow, pink and red roses. "Miss Moore?"

"Yes."

"These are for you."

Sheila took the flowers and tipped the young woman. "They're beautiful and they smell wonderful."

"Thank you."

Sheila read the card that was attached.

I know this is a hard time for you right now, but when I saw these, I thought they would brighten your day.

It was signed by Nicholas.

She leaned over and sniffed the bouquet. "You always know just what I need." Nicholas was always available to her whenever she needed him. He was the one constant in her life.

Things were great between them—the only issue was Diana.

Sheila didn't like that Nicholas allowed his ex-wife to live in his house. She didn't understand why he didn't just pay for a hotel. Zoe could've stayed with him, but Diana... she was manipulative and scheming to break up her and Nicholas. Sheila wasn't about to let that happen.

She picked up the phone to call a realtor when the idea came. She was thinking of selling the rental so why not offer it to Nicholas for Diana and Zoe. If his ex-wife intended on staying in Charleston—she should be in her own place.

Sheila would bring up the idea when Nicholas came over for dinner later. It was the perfect solution, and they could once again have a place to spend some quality time alone. Gray was home more now that he was back in school except for football practice and game nights.

Diana was already starting to be problematic for them, but Sheila was determined to find a way to get her away from Nicholas.

NICHOLAS SAUTÉED the onions and garlic, stirring every couple of minutes while Sheila placed a pot of pasta on the stove.

"You were right about Diana all along." It pained him to admit that fact, but there was no denying the truth.

A look of tenderness passed over her features. "Babe, you have no idea how much I wanted to be wrong about this." She handed him a bowl of shrimp deveined and tails off. "The white wine is to your right."

Sheila and Gray loved his shrimp scampi. So did Kiya but she was studying for a test and decided it was best to stay on campus. She'd made him promise to bring her some tomorrow for lunch.

"I have an idea," Sheila said while stirring the pasta. "My tenants moved out last week in the house on Millberry Street.

I was thinking it would be a great place for Diana and Zoe. They won't be that far from your place."

He thought it was a great idea. He wanted his ex-wife out of his home. She was always staring, giving him seductive looks, and being flirty. "Would you sell it to me?" Nicholas asked.

"Sure," Sheila responded with a smile. "It's a really nice house."

"I know that. You've always been very particular about your properties."

"I heard Zoe mention that she enjoys swimming. This house comes with a pool."

Nicholas poured the cooked shrimp into a bowl. "She's going to love that."

"And Diana?" Sheila questioned.

"It doesn't matter," he responded.

His answer was enough for her.

She checked on the pasta.

There was no need for further discussion. They had found their solution.

———

"I HAVE SOME GOOD NEWS," Nicholas announced when he entered his home four hours later.

Zoe and Diana were in the kitchen cleaning up.

"What is it?" His ex-wife asked, a grin on her face. "Did you get a promotion?"

"Nothing with the job. I bought a house for you."

Diana's smile vanished. She glanced at her daughter, then said, "A house…why would you do that?"

"I figured you ladies would be more comfortable in your own space. We can go shopping this weekend for furniture."

"That's really nice of you," Zoe said. "What does it look like?"

"It's not too far from here and it has four bedrooms. It's a two-story brick home with a large backyard. It'll be great when your brothers come."

Diana clearly didn't look pleased. "Zoe, I need to talk to your father." When they were alone, she uttered, "We don't need your pity or your handout, Nick. If you want us to leave, just say so."

"This isn't about charity," he responded. "But I do want to make sure my daughter has a home. *This is for her.*"

"All I'm hearing is that you don't want us here. Are we cramping your style? Is your girlfriend complaining about us living with you?"

Nicholas worked to keep his frustration at bay. "Diana, you need to calm down."

"You want me to be calm, yet you keep letting that woman interfere with your family."

"Keep Sheila out of this," he snapped.

Diana was taken aback.

"I apologize for my tone, but I'm tired of you blaming Sheila for everything. She's not the problem."

"Oh, but I am. Is that what you're trying to say?"

Nicholas didn't respond.

"Your silence tells me that I'm right," Diana stated.

"It's best that you and Zoe have your own space. I'll admit that it's awkward for me, especially when you're running around here trying to seduce me. You might as well give up because I'm not interested, Diana."

Chapter 16

"Mom, why are you so mad?" Zoe asked when they were alone in her room. "I think it's nice of my dad to buy us a house."

"You're missing the obvious, child," Diana snapped. "He doesn't want us here because of Sheila. She's the one behind this—I'm sure of it."

"Well, I like having our own home. This place is all *him*. There's no reflection of me or you here."

Diana dismissed her daughter's words with the wave of her hand. "I'm going to find a way to change his mind. I don't intend on leaving this house. Nick's probably found some little shack to put us in."

"He's taking us to look at the house tomorrow."

"Doesn't matter," Diana uttered. "I'm not leaving here... not without a fight."

"Why do you want to stay here?"

"This should be our home, Zoe. We're a family."

"He's my daddy, but that's it, Mom. I hardly know the man. I would hardly call us a family."

"Child, you don't know any better."

"I'm not a child and I understand exactly what happened," Zoe responded. "You had an affair."

Diana flinched at her daughter's words. "I made a mistake. I can't deny it, but I'm trying to make things right."

"Do you really think that's possible?"

"Nick loved me once. I just have to remind him of just how much."

Zoe shook her head sadly. "Mom, he's in love with Sheila."

"He only thinks he does," Diana responded. "You'll see…"

NICHOLAS LED the way into the house located in the North Charleston neighborhood of Windsor Hill. "See, you're just a stone's throw away from my place."

Sullen, Diana didn't respond.

"The grocery store, restaurants and gas station…right down the street."

"I love it," Zoe gushed. "This house is so nice."

"Why did Sheila decide to sell?" Diana asked. "I'm sure she was making a lot of money when she was renting it out. I guess she must have really wanted to get us away from you. Why is your girlfriend so insecure?"

Nicholas gave her a sharp look. "It doesn't matter why she decided to sell it. I bought it because I thought it would be perfect for you and Zoe."

"Mom, this is perfect for us. It's got four bedrooms, a screened-in patio—you know you love those, and it has a pool."

"The backyard is fully fenced," Nicholas stated. "There's even a flatscreen TV on the patio. Sheila conveyed it with the home."

"How sweet," Diana uttered.

"Mom..." Zoe said. "Just stop..."

"The pool has a new saltwater pump installed."

"Nicholas, you can stop trying to sell me on this place," Diana stated. "You've already purchased it. Whether we want to or not, we're moving in—it's a done deal."

He eyed her for a moment, then responded. "You're right. It's done."

His ex-wife wasn't happy, and she made sure to let him know, but Nicholas didn't care. He was doing what was best for everyone involved.

When they returned to his place, he said, "Diana, I'd like to speak to you alone."

"What is it, Nick?"

"What's going on with you?" he asked.

"It would've been nice if I'd been included in the decision of where my daughter and I live."

"Diana, I'm sorry if I offended you. I was focused on finding a nice place for you and Zoe that was close by."

"I appreciate what you did, but I just feel I should have been the one you were consulting with—not Sheila."

"I thought it was a good idea when she mentioned she was going to sell the house."

"So, Sheila didn't suggest it?" Diana asked.

"Well, she did mention that she thought it would work for you and Zoe."

"I knew it..."

"Don't do that," Nicholas said. "Stop trying to make Sheila the enemy because she's not."

"She doesn't like me."

"From where I'm standing, it's clear that you don't care much for her either."

"Why are we talking about this?" Diana asked. "Nothing's going to change."

"I'm hoping you and Sheila will find some common ground."

She gave a short chuckle. "Not going to happen."

"DID THEY LIKE THE HOUSE?" Sheila asked when Nicholas arrived the next day to drive her to the doctor.

"Zoe loved it, but Diana... that's another story."

She chuckled. "I'm not at all surprised."

"It's a really nice place," Nicholas stated.

"Diana doesn't like it because I sold you the house. *Plain and simple.*"

He nodded in agreement.

"That's really petty."

"I told her that it was a done deal. They're moving into that house as soon as we close."

"Don't be surprised if Diana tries to manipulate you into letting her stay with you," Sheila warned.

"She's upset right now, but Diana will come around. She wants her daughter to be happy."

"I doubt it."

"As long as Zoe's happy—that's all I care about."

"You have to also consider your ex-wife's feelings, too. If you don't, things can become problematic."

Nicholas considered her words.

Chapter 17

NICHOLAS RETURNED HOME from Sheila's house shortly after midnight. Zoe was downstairs watching television in the family room.

"Where's your mom?" he asked.

"I think she went to bed. She said she was tired." Zoe glanced over at him. "Just so you know... I really like the house. It's so perfect for us."

"I agree," Nicholas responded with a smile. "I know you like to swim so when Sheila told me it came with a pool—I knew it was the one for you and your mother."

Zoe turned off the television. "I guess I'll go up to my room. I have an appointment with an admissions counselor at nine in the morning. I hope all my credits transfer over."

"It'll all work out."

Nicholas made sure the house was locked up and secure

before making his way to the second level where the bedrooms were located.

He headed to his room.

Nicholas met Diana in the hallway. "I thought you'd gone to bed already."

"I was waiting up for you."

"What are you up to?" he asked.

"Being here with you has been wonderful," she responded. "It reminded me of the old days. We were so good together."

"That's not how I remember it. I remember coming home one day and finding you gone. No note. *Nothing*."

Keeping her voice low, she responded, "Nick, I'm so sorry. I really need you to forgive me. We have a daughter together. I thought you'd be happy about this. We wanted a family, remember. Well, you have your family now—only now you want us to leave."

"Diana, you're moving into a place of your own. You and Zoe won't be that far from here. It's probably a ten-minute drive."

"This is Sheila's idea," she uttered. "That woman doesn't want us here. She's trying to destroy our family, Nick. I don't know why you can't see it."

"Diana, I appreciate you telling me about Zoe, but there can't be anything between you and me. *She* is my family."

"You loved me once. You can't deny that our marriage started off like a fairy tale."

"We all know not all fairy tale marriages end up... happily ever after."

Diana narrowed her eyes and clenched her lips tightly.

"I'm sorry. It's been a long day and I'm tired. I'm going to bed."

She was stumped. Diana didn't know which felt worse: Steve cheating on her or being rejected by her ex-husband.

Diana's marriage with Steve had been rudely interrupted by a 120-pound, five-foot, six-inch secret with long blond hair and blue eyes. Her husband had no idea she'd known about his mistress for six months. After everything she'd sacrificed to be with Steve... he had the nerve to be unfaithful. However, her marriage was pretty much over before the woman ever entered the picture. Diana hadn't allowed her husband to touch her since his father died and he allowed his sister to walk in and take the money and the business without a fight.

It was bad enough that she was being dissed by high society and underestimated because of Steve. Diana wasn't perfect, but she owned who she was, and she didn't apologize for it. If she'd stayed with Nicholas...things would've turned out very different. Steve made good money, but he lacked class and sophistication. He wasn't even man enough to contest his father's will.

Diana wanted Nicholas. She regretted being unfaithful and leaving him, but she couldn't undo the past. "I understand why you're being guarded, but Nick—all I want is another chance. *We have a daughter together.*"

"She is eighteen years old," Nicholas stated. "Not a little girl. Zoe is old enough to understand that we both love her, but we haven't been a couple since before she was born."

"I don't want Sheila's bad habits influencing my daughter. I know all about her."

"She's not the same person she used to be," Nicholas responded. "You claim you're no longer the woman you were... why is it so hard to believe that Sheila has changed?"

"I never stopped loving you, Nick."

"I'm sorry but I don't feel the same way." He opened the door to his room. "Goodnight Diana."

"How DID last night go with Nicholas?" Zoe asked her mother when she entered the kitchen. Diana was making scrambled eggs and bacon.

"I was sent to my room."

"Huh? Mom, what exactly did you do?"

"It's not worth talking about."

Zoe closed her eyes, groaning. "I can't believe you. Did you try to seduce him?"

Diana stared at her daughter. "I will do whatever I have to do to make sure we get what we need."

"Mom, you don't have to force yourself on him. I'll get a job... two jobs if I have to—I can sit out the rest of this semester."

"The only reason nothing happened between us last night is because Nick's still dealing with what happened back then." She placed the strips of cooked bacon on a plate. "I really want you to do something for me, dear."

"What do you need?" asked Zoe.

"I need you to talk to your dad… maybe you can get him to understand how important it is for us to build our life together as a family."

Shaking her head, Zoe took a sip of her orange juice. "I'm not doing that. He's too caught up with Sheila Moore. I'm not getting involved."

"We need his help."

"No, we don't, Mom."

"Zoe, I'm doing all this for you," Diana stated. "You are Nick's only child. He *should* want to take care of you."

"Maybe in time he will," she responded. "Let it be his decision."

Zoe kissed her mother's cheek, then stood up and stretched. "I'm going to check on my dad, but I'm not gonna try to manipulate him."

Her mother's teary eyes caused a stir of emotion inside her. This was both frightening and intriguing for Zoe.

Just as she headed toward the stairs, Nicholas was coming down. "Good morning."

He smiled. "Good morning, Zoe. What are your plans for today?"

"I was hoping we'd be able to hang out after your last class."

"Why don't you come with me now? You can sit in my class or wait in my office for me—whichever you prefer."

"I'd love to watch you teach."

Throughout the day, Zoe watched her father interact with Kiya. A thread of jealousy washed over her. She was his student, but outside of the classroom, Nicholas seemed more like he was her dad. She had to remind herself that he'd known Kiya longer than he'd known her—they had already established their relationship.

"Are you okay?" Nicholas asked, bringing her out of her reverie.

She looked at him and smiled. "I'm fine."

"You sure? Zoe, I want you to know you can talk to me about anything."

"How do you feel about having a daughter?" she blurted. "I know you and my mother talked about it, but I need to hear it for myself."

"I'm overjoyed. I've always wanted a family."

"It looks like you have one with Sheila," Zoe stated. "I'm not sure there's room for me."

"Of course, there's room for you," Nicholas said. "I hate that I wasn't able to be there for you—if I'd known… nothing could've kept me away. You're extremely important to me and I want to get to know you. As for Sheila and her kids—they are also a significant part of my life. I hope you will get to know them and form your own opinions. I know how your mother feels about Sheila."

"Mom doesn't make my decisions for me," Zoe said. "She's not really a bad person, you know. My mother."

"I know," Nicholas responded. "She and I love you very much. We want the best for you. I wasn't there when you were growing up, but I'm here now and I'm not going anywhere. I give you my word, Zoe. I'm hoping you'll consider attending the university. You could start the winter semester."

"I'll think about it."

"You can attend any college you'd like, Zoe. I'll take care of your tuition."

"I want to make something clear. I don't want you in my life because of your money or fame. I just want to get to know my dad. I can work, get student loans—I'll find a way to fund my education."

"Sweetheart, you don't have to do any of that. Zoe, this is something I *want* to do for you."

She smiled. "You've been wonderful to us. The house... college... thank you for everything."

"It's the least I could do."

"Dad... I mean Steve... he's always been a great father. I hate that my brothers and I live in separate homes. I wish he'd just forgive my mom. I really want them to work things out."

"So do I," Nicholas said.

"I'm glad we had this time alone," Zoe stated. I really wanted to hear your thoughts on everything."

"How was your day with your father?" Diana asked.

"I had a great time with him," Zoe answered. "He showed me around campus; I sat in his class—he's a great teacher."

"And Sheila's daughter?"

"She was friendly. We ate lunch together and she introduced me to some of her friends."

"Did you mention anything about us staying here in Charleston?"

"I didn't. Besides, I'm sure she already knows." Zoe met her mother's gaze. "I think having our own house is a good idea. Nicholas needs his space, Mom."

"We are his family."

"You're married to Steve, or did you forget? I have two younger brothers who need their mother."

"I haven't forgotten anything, Zoe. I miss my boys like crazy, but Steve... he's really angry and I'm trying to give him a chance to cool off."

"Do you still love him?"

"I do but not in the same way I love Nick. I'm sorry I've put you in such a difficult position, my darling."

"Mom, do something for me..."

"What is it?" Diana asked.

"Stop fighting this move. Nicholas has been very generous. He bought a house for us. I'm grateful. You should be, too. Besides, I think I'd like to stay here in Charleston. My dad said I could attend any university I want, but he'd like me to consider his school."

"See... that is coming together nicely."

"I'm not going to use the man for his money," Zoe stated.

"I'm only getting you what you deserve as a Washington."

"Mama, I'm a Winston. Just a Washington by blood."

"Oh, that's gonna change, sugar. You will carry your father's name. I'm working on that."

Chapter 18

ZOE WAS in her room packing up the last of her clothes.

Diana was sullen as she sat on the couch downstairs waiting for her daughter.

"Are you ready?" Nicholas asked from the doorway.

"Sure," she uttered.

"Everything is in the truck. The furniture is scheduled to be delivered this afternoon." He'd purchased bedroom sets, a sectional sofa and a dining room table and chairs. Diana refused to go shopping with them, so Nicholas allowed Zoe to pick out the furnishings.

She didn't respond.

"Diana, please don't act this way. I'm only ten minutes away. I'm not going to abandon Zoe. I don't know why you'd even think that."

"The whole point of us coming here was for our daughter

to get to know you. I don't see how we can accomplish that by living apart."

"Zoe is welcome to stay over here anytime she wants, Diana." He was not going to let her put a guilt trip on him.

"We'll see how much she appreciates what you've done."

"Our daughter seems happy enough about this move."

"Don't you dare presume to know the child I've raised all these years."

Nicholas was imposing at his full height, which had to be a good foot taller than her five-foot-six-inch frame. He strode toward her with such purpose her mouth suddenly went dry. Then he leaned down and whispered, "Diana, I'm not going to fight with you about this. You're a grown woman. You can live wherever you want. Zoe can move in with me. I can rent the house out or sell it. I'm not forcing you to do anything you don't want to do. All I tried to do was find a suitable solution that would work for all of us."

"I just think it's better for us to stay here."

"Not going to happen."

The ebb and flow of a shiver brought the tiny hairs on Diana's arms to attention just from the look Nicholas gave her. He gave her little time to linger on her body's reaction and walked away again toward the kitchen.

Diana opened her mouth, then closed it again before she said something very unladylike.

Count to ten, Diana and don't even think about tasing him with the taser in her purse.

Once the moment passed, she called upon her rational self to stay calm. She could tell by his expression that Nicholas wasn't in the mood for one of her tantrums. He'd made up his mind and they were moving. There was nothing she could do to change her circumstances.

Nick, you may have won this round, but I'm not done, Diana wanted to shout but kept her thoughts to herself. For now, she would play nice—she didn't want to end up alienating him.

After Nicholas left, Diana looked at her daughter. "This wasn't how it was supposed to be, Zoe."

"Mama, I'm good...no, I'm great. This house is beautiful, and we have a pool. You've always wanted a house with a pool. We get to live here. Why can't you be happy about this?"

"I'm not unhappy, Zoe. Not about the house really. I don't like that Sheila had something to do with it. I would've preferred Nick discuss our housing plans with me."

"I don't see why it's such a big deal."

"That's because you're only eighteen." Diana glanced around. "I guess we need to get started. These boxes aren't gonna unpack themselves."

"I love my new bedroom," Zoe gushed. "It's just as nice as the one I have at my dad's house."

Diana glanced around her surroundings. She wasn't happy at all.

———————————

"You look tired," Sheila stated when Nicholas came to her house.

"I am," he confirmed. "But Zoe and Diana are all moved in."

"I'm sure your ex-wife really hates me now."

"No, I think all of her anger and hatred is directly toward me," Nicholas responded. "I thought what I was doing was a good thing, especially since Diana told me they had nowhere to live, and she didn't have money."

"You didn't have to do what you did, Nicholas. It's a very generous gift. She should be grateful."

"I think she really wanted to live with me."

"That's because she was hoping to get you back into bed. Her goal was to seduce you or have you fall back in love with her. She wants the three of you to be one big happy family. I get it, but I'm not going anywhere," Sheila stated. "Unless you tell me she's the one you want."

Nicholas frowned. "That's never going to happen."

"Maybe you should have a conversation with her husband," Sheila suggested. "I'm sure he can shed light on this situation. There are too many unanswered questions."

"I thought about it, but I think Diana's right on one point. I'm the last person Steve will want to have a conversation with."

Zoe invited Nicholas to have dinner with them three days later. He didn't want to disappoint his daughter, so he accepted the invite. There was still tension between him and Diana, but he hoped to keep the evening a pleasant one.

"Dinner was delicious, Zoe," Nicholas said in an effort to ease the awkwardness. "You're very talented in the kitchen."

"I guess it's a gift I inherited from Mom." She glanced over at her mother who seemed to be concentrating on the food on her plate.

Nicholas agreed. Diana was a great cook.

"Mom…"

Diana glanced up. "Yeah sweetie…"

"Everything okay? You haven't said a word."

"I'm fine."

"How's the food?"

"It's delicious, Zoe. You did a great job." Diana dabbed her mouth with her napkin. "Since you cooked, I'll clean the kitchen. This way you can enjoy quality time with your father."

"Thanks, Mom."

"Anything for *you*, sugar."

"Mom's never been this quiet before," Zoe said in a low voice when they settled in the living room. She searched for a movie to watch. "I wonder if she's feeling well."

"I think she's still upset with me," Nicholas responded. "It's fine. We'll work it out eventually."

"To be honest, I like spending time with you—just the two of us," Zoe stated while Diana was cleaning up the kitchen. "But I was thinking that we should invite Sheila to join us sometime. I guess I should probably get to know Kiya and Gray better, too."

Nicholas broke into a grin. "I'd like that."

"I had a feeling you would."

"Zoe... there's something you should know. When the time is right, I plan on proposing to Sheila," he announced. "I'd like to know how you feel about it."

"You really love her, don't you?"

Nicholas nodded. "I do."

"I want you to be happy, Nicholas."

"No pressure, but it's okay if you want to call me dad, Zoe. I'd be honored if you decide to do so."

"I didn't know if it would be weird for you."

He embraced her. "Not as all."

"Thanks, Dad."

"So, what movie did you choose?" Nicholas asked.

Chapter 19

"LET'S PLAY UNO," Gray suggested.

"I'd rather play Spades," Kiya stated.

"Should we flip a coin?"

Laughing, her daughter asked, "Really Mama?"

"Do you have a better suggestion to solve this dilemma?" Sheila questioned.

"Which do you prefer?"

Leaning back against the cushions on her sofa, she responded, "Gray, I'm actually a bit tired. Whatever we play needs to be a quick game."

"Maybe we should just call it a night," Kiya suggested. "I'll come home next Friday, and we'll pick it up from here."

"Isn't it game weekend?' Sheila asked.

"It's on Saturday."

"I'd like to go," Gray said.

"I already got you a ticket, little brother. I'm coming

Friday to see you play," Kiya stated. "Now don't embarrass me out there."

"Coach says I'm the best wide receiver on the team."

"Even the best can have a bad night," Sheila interjected. "Just go out there and play all four quarters. Give it your all, then leave it on the field."

She slowly rose to her feet. "I'm going to bed."

Kiya studied her mother. "Are you sure you're okay?"

Trembling from exhaustion, Sheila answered, "I think I over did it earlier when I was making the baked ziti. I made three pans to put in the freezer."

"Yum…" Gray muttered. "I've been wanting some ziti."

"I know," Sheila responded. "That's why I went on and made so much of it."

"I'm taking one of them back to school with me," Kiya announced. "Just so you know."

Sheila chuckled, then kissed each of her children. "I'll see you in the morning."

"Goodnight, Mama," they said in unison.

In her bedroom, Sheila changed into a nightgown and climbed into her bed, wondering how Nicholas enjoyed his evening with Zoe and Diana. They'd both agreed they would make this night about their children. However, he would also have to contend with his ex-wife. As far as she's concerned, people are exes for a reason. From what Nicholas told her, Diana left him to be with another man. She'd admitted this as well.

What's changed to make her so interested in Nicholas now?

Was it because he was a struggling writer back then and

she was involved with the heir apparent to Winston Electronics? According to her research, Steve Winston had been left out of his father's will. Her gut instinct told Sheila that Diana's sudden estrangement from her husband had more to do with his financial situation than anything else, but she couldn't prove it.

Zoe looked nothing like the Winston family, but that didn't mean he wasn't her biological father. It also didn't mean that she wasn't fathered by Nicholas either. Only a DNA test could provide the truth.

She was his daughter—Sheila knew this is what Nicholas believed. She hoped Zoe was indeed his child. Her major frustration was the way he handled his ex-wife. He was much too nice and allowed Diana to get away with her shenanigans. Sheila wanted him to call her out on her mess. She knew he didn't want to upset Zoe by bickering with her mother, but she wasn't a little girl—she was practically a grown woman.

I'm sure she's witnessed an argument or two between Diana and Steve. That witch is trying to lay a guilt trip on him. Zoe is not that fragile.

Sheila was trying to stay in her lane, but it was a struggle for her to sit back and watch the man she loved being manipulated.

———

"TONIGHT, it's just about you and me," Nicholas told Sheila. "No children..."

"No *Diana*," she interjected.

They left the restaurant where they had eaten dinner and was in the car headed to see a play at the Performing Arts Theater.

"Sweetheart, what are you thinking about right now?" Nicholas asked.

"I would give anything to have my mother back with me."

"I miss her, too."

They arrived at the theater twenty minutes later.

Once they were seated, Nicholas reached over and took her by the hand, giving it a light squeeze.

She held it as if holding on for dear life. A delicious shudder heated her body at his touch. She closed her eyes and concentrated on keeping her breathing even. The warmth of Nicholas's body captivated her. Sheila felt the heat of desire wash over her like waves.

He smelled good, like warm skin and amber and spices, and when she leaned her head against him, his shoulder felt very solid. "I always feel so safe with you," she whispered.

"I will always protect you and the children," Nicholas whispered back.

The show started.

Every now and then Sheila's eyes would travel to his lips. She wanted so much to experience the touch of his mouth against hers. She needed to feel again—to make the numbness of grief go away.

Nicholas met her gaze, then placed an arm around her shoulders. The warmth building in the pit of her stomach coupled with the way she felt under his protection ignited something more.

Their gazes locked as his fingers were intertwined with hers. For a long minute they simply stared at each other.

Intermission was over. They returned their attention back to the show.

At the end of the evening, Nicholas and Sheila returned to her house to have a cup of herbal tea and a slice of lemon pound cake with fresh strawberries.

They stayed up talking until well past midnight.

"Sheila Moore," he said, so softly it was barely more than a whisper. "I'm crazy in love with you." Then he leaned forward and pressed his lips to hers.

The world suddenly stood still.

Sheila's heart stuttered in her chest, and it was like she'd forgotten how to breathe.

Nicholas's mouth moved against hers once more and heat exploded in her belly. In that fraction of a second, Sheila knew how it would be when they finally made love—it would be a fiery passion.

She knew Nicholas wanted to abstain until marriage and though it was a struggle at times for Sheila—she wouldn't push to change his mindset. In fact, she admired him for his ability to remain abstinent all these years. Nicholas desired to honor God with his body.

Reluctantly, she was the one who pulled away. "It's getting late. You should probably leave. You have an early class in the morning... or actually in a few hours, babe."

"I want you, Sheila."

"I want to be with you, too. But you know that can't happen," she said. "I refuse to be the one who causes you to break your vow of abstinence. I stay in enough trouble with the Lord on my own."

He laughed. "In my mind I've broken my vow so many times already."

"Babe, that's between you and the Lord."

Nicholas assisted her up from the sofa.

She escorted him to the door.

"Saturday, Diane and Zoe have plans, so we're going to the waterfront," he announced. "We'll have a nice picnic in the park."

"Sounds perfect," Sheila responded with a smile. "Kiya and Gray are going to a football game. It will just be the two of us."

SHEILA WOKE up early Saturday morning, stretching and yawning. She'd had a restful night's sleep—the first since her mother died.

A glance at the clock told her it was seven-thirty a.m. It was like waking up on a bright sunny day even though she'd yet to open the curtains. Not only was she rested but thanks to Nicholas, her dreams had been full of kisses and passionate embraces. She was starting the day on a high.

She coupled the lazy smile on her face with another stretch.

Sheila went downstairs and made breakfast for her and Gray.

"Why don't you come to the game with us?" he asked.

"I have a date with Nicholas."

"Oh, okay. Have a good time."

"You, too," Sheila said, "and don't go around lying about your age."

"Older girls don't bring a lot of drama like the girls my age."

"I need you to focus on your education, Gray."

"Yes ma'am."

"Uh huh… you're not listening to a word I've said."

"C'mon Mama… I hear you."

Nicholas arrived promptly at noon to pick her up.

They headed to the waterfront park to spend an afternoon relaxing in the sun like several other couples around them. The clouds that had been steadily moving in to spoil her day began to dissipate until her smile was as bright as the September sun shining overhead.

They walked around the park, past families playing ball games, couples stretched out together on the green and dog walkers trying to get their enthusiastic charges under control.

"How about here?" Nicholas found a shady spot beneath a huge tree.

"It's perfect."

Nicholas stripped off his jacket to spread it out on the grass.

"There's really no need to ruin your jacket on my account." Although Sheila appreciated the gesture, she could only imagine the cost of getting grass stains out of the expensive light grey fabric.

The tangle of branches above their heads shielded them from the glare of the afternoon sun. Nicholas lay down beside her, putting the other half of his suit at risk by lying on the grass. He kicked off his shoes and socks. "That's better."

Sheila watched him with amusement at how quickly he'd been able to switch off from being a published author to just being Nicholas regular guy.

"Why don't you make yourself comfortable?" she teased.

"If I do that, the shirt and jeans would be off too, and I'd be lying here in my boxers."

His flirty wink coupled with the picture he'd painted in her mind conspired to raise her temperature so much she might as well have been sitting in direct sunlight.

Sheila began fanning herself with her hand.

Nicholas chuckled.

"Are you hungry?" he pointed to the picnic basket.

"Yes, I am."

He pulled out a container of pasta salad, blackened chicken and veggie wheat wraps and a container of fruit.

With the plastic cutlery provided, Sheila helped herself to the tomato and basil pasta salad. Nicholas offered her one of the sandwich wraps and she took it. She washed her lunch down with a bottle of water.

"I'm stuffed." Nicholas lay back with his arms folded beneath his head. He tossed the empty wrapper from his lunch back into the bag. He retrieved a package of apple wedges and toffee dipping sauce.

"Someone has a sweet tooth."

"I thought we needed something decadent." Nicholas dipped his head, his lips brushing hers.

Sheila watched him with fascination as he munched on the apple slice. There shouldn't have been anything erotic in the act, yet Sheila found it incredibly sexy. She felt like Nicholas was slowly seducing her with his mouth.

His eyes didn't leave hers. Her heart seemed to grow twice its size to accommodate the amount of love she had for this gorgeous man.

She fanned herself to cool off her heated body.

The sound of chattering children somewhere nearby filtered into Sheila's consciousness, forcing her to think about something other than the sexy man beside her.

Chapter 20

SHEILA DECIDED to do some shopping after her doctor's appointment. She and Valerie entered her favorite store downtown.

"Sheila Moore..."

She turned around to come face-to-face with Diana. "Hello *Mrs. Winston*. I didn't expect to see you here in light of everything that's been going on." Sheila was under the impression that Diana was broke, but here she was with an arm full of clothing.

"I'm just doing a little window shopping."

"I see."

"I thought I'd try on a few pieces—just to see how this brand looks on my body. When you're curvy like me—you can't wear certain styles."

Bored with the conversation, Sheila said, "Well enjoy..." She was ready to go about her business.

"I'm glad we ran into each other," Diana said.

Sheila stopped in her tracks. "Why is that?"

"I feel we should have a conversation woman to woman."

"And why is that?' Sheila asked again. "You and I have nothing to discuss."

"We have a lot to talk about. For the time being, we gonna be in each other's lives."

"I don't agree. Zoe will be in my life, but I don't have to deal with the baby mama."

"Oh, but you do…" Diana said. "I'm not going anywhere. Actually, I have you to thank for that. If you hadn't sold that house to Nick—maybe, we wouldn't still be in town."

"You don't fool me," Sheila responded. "You had no intentions of leaving the moment you showed up in Charleston."

Diana gave a short chuckle. "You think you know me, but you don't. I will say this—I'm not one to play with."

"Neither am I," Sheila countered. "The difference between you and me—you're trying to creep in the back door while I'm the type of person who will walk straight through the front. I don't throw rocks and hide my hand."

Diana inched closer to Sheila. "I don't make it a habit of disrespecting disabled people, but I'm not gon' let you talk to me any kind of way."

She didn't back down. "I didn't want to talk to you at all, Diana."

Valerie walked up to the ladies, saying, "Miss Moore, let's get going."

"Yes, let's..." she responded. "I'm done here."

"I CAN'T STAND that uppity little troll..." Diana huffed when she entered the house. "I ran into Sheila Moore at this little boutique downtown."

"Why were you there?" Zoe asked. "I thought we didn't have any money."

She placed her shopping bags near the staircase. "I just picked up a couple of things I needed. They were on sale."

"We need to save our money, Mom."

She placed a gentle hand to her daughter's cheek. "Nicholas isn't gonna let us go without, sugar. He gave me a credit card for emergencies."

"You need to give it back to him," Zoe uttered. "We don't need any handouts. Why aren't you looking for a job or something, Mom?"

"Excuse me?"

"A job... there's no reason why you can't work."

"I worked enough when I was married to Nicholas. I worked two jobs so he could work on that dang book. He owes me, Zoe and I'm gonna make sure I get what's due me."

"What you're doing is wrong?'

"Some days I'm not sure whose child you are... you're nothing like me." Diana danced up the stairs with her purchases.

"I LOVE school but I'm so glad to be on break right now," Kiya said. "Those classes were kicking my tail." She and her mother were getting manicures and pedicures at their favorite nail spa.

"I felt the same way when I started college. It may feel a bit overwhelming right now, but you'll be fine, sweetie."

"Miss Val told me y'all ran into Diana," Kiya announced.

"We did and it was uneventful. She did what she usually does—try to get under my skin. It didn't work."

"I'm glad her daughter is nothing like her," Kiya stated.

"Me, too," Sheila responded. "Two of them… now that would be a nightmare."

"How do you think things will go with Diana at Nicholas's house on Thanksgiving?"

"He'll keep her in check," Sheila said. "If he doesn't—his aunt and uncle will. I'm not happy she's going to be there, but I have to stay in my lane. This is Nicholas's house. He can invite whomever he pleases."

"Are things between the two of you still good?' Kiya inquired.

"Yes. Things are great. I know I'm the one he wants and I trust him completely."

"You know she's not gonna give up, Mama."

"Neither am I," Sheila responded.

Nails done, they headed home.

Kiya settled in the family room to watch a movie while Sheila headed to her bedroom. "I'm going to do some reading before dinner."

She wasn't worried about Nicholas at all. Sheila just wasn't in the mood for any of Diana's continued attempts to get under her skin. She didn't want to revert back to her old ways, but his ex-wife wasn't making it easy on her.

Chapter 21

"WILL you be having Thanksgiving dinner here with me or with your father and Sheila?" Diana asked Zoe when she walked into the kitchen and grabbed an apple.

"Why can't I do both?"

"I guess you can—it's up to you, but it really shouldn't be a choice. I'm so tired of him letting Sheila make the rules." She banged her fist on the counter. "I just want her to disappear."

"Mom... what's wrong with you? What are you talking about? You act like Nicholas can't think for himself."

"What's wrong is that I'm tired of Nick treating me as if I'm not a member of this family. He's trying to appease Sheila."

"The only connection between you and my dad is me."

"You think I don't know that?"

"Then stop trying to break them up."

"If they're so in love—I wouldn't be able to come between them."

"That's just it. I don't want you to try," Zoe said. "Just let them be. I'll be in my room if you need me."

Diana walked over to the sofa in the family room and sat down. *I should be at the family dinner*, she thought silently. *I'm not letting Sheila win this round. I'm going to the dinner. Nicholas is too polite to ask me to leave and the witch can't make me leave because it's not her house.*

Eventually she'll learn not to mess with Diana Washington Winston.

The Washington family rotated holidays, so it was Nicholas' turn to host Thanksgiving in Charleston this year and Christmas would be in Brunswick.

"Toya, can I call you back?" Kiya asked, on speakerphone with her friend. "My mother will never let me forget it, if I screw up this white chocolate bread pudding."

She ended the call.

Sheila strolled into the kitchen. "Oh sweetie... you're making my favorite."

"I hope Professor Washington's aunt and uncle will like it."

"If they have a sweet tooth, I'm sure they will enjoy it. What can I do to help?"

"Do you mind separating the egg whites?" Kiya asked.

"Not at all." Sheila glanced over her shoulder. "Where is everybody?"

"They went to the grocery store. Professor Washington's mom didn't think there was enough food. Oh, I'm on turkey duty. It's been in the oven for three hours now."

"Nicholas's family tends to cook for an army during the holidays," Sheila said with a chuckle. "I've never seen anything like it."

"That's because we don't come from a big family, I guess."

"Where's Gray?"

"He went with Professor Washington," Kiya announced.

Sheila retrieved the eggs from the refrigerator and sat down at the counter to separate the six needed for the recipe. She heard the door open and close. "Nicholas..." she called out.

"Sorry to disappoint you," Diana said as she strolled into the kitchen carrying a bag of groceries. "It's just me."

"Nicholas and his mother are at the store," Sheila announced. "Did he know you were coming by?"

"I'm making two cakes; a lemon and a key lime at *Nick's* request."

"Is there something wrong with the oven at the house?"

"No, it's fine actually. I just happen to like this oven better."

"My daughter's going to need it. Also, the turkey is already in the oven so there isn't space for two cakes."

"This isn't your house, Sheila."

"You're right, it isn't, but Nicholas and I... we're together.

We're a couple, Diana and you need to deal with it. You can't just run over here anytime you want."

Diana laughed. "Do you really want to do this now?"

Kiya bent down to peek into the oven, checking on the turkey.

"We'll just wait and see what Nicholas has to say about this." Sheila poured a cup of sugar into a mixture of egg yolks, melted white chocolate and whipping cream. Stirring, she said, "This is almost ready, sweetie. Have you sliced up the French bread yet?"

"Is there anything I can do to assist?" Diana offered. "What is it you're trying to make?"

Ignoring her, Kiya said, "I've already put it in the pan, Mama."

"My daughter's planning to make a white chocolate bread pudding. It's a recipe passed down from her late grandmother."

"Your mother?"

"No, this comes from her biological grandmother."

"Well, I certainly can't wait to sample this bread pudding when it's done."

Sheila released a short sigh of relief when Nicholas returned.

He was clearly surprised to see Diana. "I didn't expect you until later for dinner."

His aunt Lily Belle strode into the kitchen with purpose. She stopped in her tracks when she saw Diana.

"Hey *Auntie*…" Diana cooed. "I've missed you so much. Happy Thanksgiving…"

"Oh really?" Lily Belle questioned. "I sho' wouldn't known since I never heard a word from you. I still got the same phone number I had back when you were married to Nicholas."

Diana's expression changed to one of shame. "I was too embarrassed to call you."

"Now that I believe."

"What are you doing here?" Nicholas asked.

"I came over to bake the cakes you asked me to make."

"What cakes?' he asked, perplexed.

"Is something wrong with your oven?" Lily Belle asked.

Diana lifted her chin in defiance. "I like the way his oven bakes."

"Well, we got a lot of cooking to do over here so there's no room," Lily Belle stated.

Sheila bit back her amusement.

"I guess I'll take my stuff and go home," Diana huffed. "If it doesn't come out right—don't blame me."

"Ain't nobody else to blame for that," Lily Belle uttered. "A good cook knows how to adapt in any kitchen. We'll see you when it's time for dinner."

"WHERE HAVE YOU BEEN?" Zoe asked.

"I went over to Nick's to bake the cakes. His aunt just basically threw me out."

"What's wrong with the oven here?"

"I wish people would stop asking me that," Diana uttered.

"This is my first Thanksgiving with my dad and his family. Mom, please don't ruin it for me."

"Zoe, I'm not trying to ruin anything. I'm doing all this for you, sugar. I want the entire Washington family to fall in love with you."

"You also want their forgiveness," her daughter responded.

"Yeah, I do. I need them to give me a second chance. My grandma used to say that time waits for no one. She's right. This is probably the only opportunity I'll ever have to make things right between me and Nick. I'm not gonna miss my shot, Zoe."

"Even if it means hurting Sheila and her kids?"

"I don't care about them," Diana responded. "I only care about you."

"So, it won't bother you to hurt Nicholas then? He loves Sheila and her children."

"If he loved her so much back then... why did they break up?"

"I don't know."

"They broke up once—it can happen again." Diana grinned. "All they need is a little nudge."

"You need to stay out of their relationship," Zoe advised. "Mom, you're gonna be the one who gets hurt."

"Sugar, you really don't know your mother, do you?"

Chapter 22

LILY BELLE PULLED Sheila off to a corner in the dining room. "You don't ever let another woman, ex-wife, ex-anything in your kitchen. Heck, you don't let 'em in your house if you can help it."

"This isn't my house, Mrs. Reynolds."

"Chile pleeze..." Lily Belle waved her hand in dismissal. "If you saw any type of pest—you'd get it outta here wouldn't you?"

"I would," she responded. "But this situation is different. Diana is the mother of your great niece."

"Well... you right about that. She does have a child, but whether my nephew's the father... he needs to have one of them DNA tests done. Then we'll know for sure."

"You have doubts?"

"I do," Lily Belle confessed. "Pete—that's my husband... we told Nicholas this when he first called to tell us about Zoe.

I could tell he was a bit disappointed in our reaction, but I know Diana. Know the whole family and she was never my choice for him. Those folks don't know the meaning of being faithful. Her daddy got chiren' all over Brunswick… I hear he got some in Darien, too. Her mama had a baby for her husband's best friend—while she was still married. When Diana ran off—I wasn't surprised. I told Nicholas I suspected she was cheating on him back then." Lowering her voice, she said, "Once when I was visiting them, I found a bottle of antibiotics. They were for a venereal disease."

"Did Nicholas know?"

"No and I didn't have the heart to tell him. I had a sit down with Diana though. I told her if I heard tell of her messing around on my nephew—I was gonna tell him everything. I know she had an abortion before she and Nicholas married. Her mama slipped up and told me about that."

"Why would she abort his baby?" Sheila asked.

"I'm not sure it was even his child."

"Oh wow…"

"I'm only telling you this because I want you to know exactly who you're dealing with. We've all made mistakes and we have our own skeletons in the closets, but we're supposed to grow and learn—not keep burying our sins. We have to own them and just do better."

Sheila nodded in agreement. "I've definitely made my share of mistakes. I don't judge Diana, but I'm also not going to play these games with her. I know she wants Nicholas back. I don't know that she's ever accept that he's moved on. He loves me and I love him."

"She won't have a choice."

The timer on the stove sounded. Kiya opened the door to the oven and peeked inside. "The turkey's ready, I think."

Nicholas's sister, Amara checked on it. "It's done. While the bread pudding and mac and cheese is in the oven, I'll heat up the greens."

Carrying the pan of bread pudding, Kiya moved around her and stuck it into the hot oven. Amara handed her the pan of macaroni and cheese which she stuck inside.

Kiya set the timer.

While the bread pudding was in the oven, Kiya sat down on one of the bar stools and began reading.

"Your chiren' are well-raised and so helpful," Lily Belle said.

"I can't complain," Sheila stated. "They're great kids considering everything they went through at such a young age."

"Nicholas says you're a wonderful mother."

"They make it so easy."

"How do you feel about Nicholas having a child—if it turns out that Zoe is really his daughter?"

"I'm thrilled for him. He's always wanted to be a father and I'm not able to give him a child. It's nice that he has a biological daughter."

"I hope and pray Diana's telling the truth. Lawd knows, I certainly do."

"So do I," Sheila said. "Nicholas would be crushed if he finds that Zoe isn't really his daughter. It would devastate them both."

Diana returned a couple of hours later. This time Zoe was with her.

Amara brought out a tray of mini crab cakes while Kiya placed a tray of deviled eggs on the table for them to nibble on. Nicholas placed the arrangement of assorted cheeses, salami, pepperoni and crackers prepared by Sheila next to the eggs.

Diana sashayed about as if she were the lady of the house. Every now and then, she'd glance over at Sheila with that fake smile of hers.

Unbothered, she didn't allow the woman to get to her. Sheila understood the type of person Diana was and she wasn't going to let her get under her skin.

Not today.

Not ever.

"Now who made this?" she asked about every item, refusing to eat anything cooked by Sheila.

"Zoe's mom is really a drama queen," Kiya whispered.

"Yes, she is…" she responded.

This was going to be a long dinner.

"I APPRECIATE the way you handle yourself around Diana," Nicholas told her as they stood outside on the patio watching the moon and star gazing. "I saw what she was doing and I'm going to have a talk with her."

"It's not worth it," Sheila responded.

"I'm tired of her acting out like some jealous or bitter ex-wife. She doesn't have the right."

"Just ignore her like I do, babe. It bothers her more that she can't really bait me into an all-out fight."

"I don't want her to upset you."

"She's not," she said. "Don't get me wrong. She irritates me like a bad rash, but I refuse to let her get the best of me."

A look of tenderness passed over his features. "I love you."

"I love you, too."

Sheila glimpsed Diana standing at the patio door, watching them. She slipped her arms around his neck and kissed him. He matched her passion kiss for kiss.

She smiled in triumph when the woman stormed off. She was gone when they returned inside the house.

"I can't believe she just up and left like that," Nicholas said.

"Maybe she just couldn't take the heat."

POSITIONED ON A LADDER, Nicholas tugged on the string of miniature teardrop-shaped outdoor lights that Gray was feeding up to him. He'd promised Sheila that he'd help them with the Christmas decorations.

When he was done, Nicholas showered and changed. He and Sheila were going to the mall. She wanted to do some gift shopping while she felt well enough to do so.

Nicholas grabbed Sheila's hand as they stepped off the escalator, pulling her to a halt.

"Will you go to Brunswick with me for Christmas?"

"I don't know if I can do that."

"Sheila, you could if you wanted to, so what's keeping you from saying yes. Tell me."

A woman with two young children in tow came off the moving stairway behind them and Sheila moved out of the way, not answering.

"Sweetheart, come home with me. Everyone is expecting to see you and the kids."

Sheila stared hard at a display of mannequins in colorful parkas and hoods in the window of one of the stores. Maybe if it were just them and her children, things might be different, but Diana and Zoe were going to be there too. She didn't have the mental capacity to spend another holiday with that woman.

Nicholas moved up behind her. "Is it because Diana is coming?"

She nodded. "I have to be honest with you. Nicholas, I can't stand being in the same room with her. She's trying really hard to insert herself back into your life and you're letting her do it—that's what so frustrating for me."

"She's the mother of my daughter, Sheila. This is new territory for me, but you know I have boundaries in place when it comes to Diana."

"I do realize that, Nicholas. But here's the thing... Zoe's not a baby. She is almost nineteen years old. You should be able to have a relationship with your daughter independent of her mother. This isn't jealousy talking. I know the type of woman Diana is because that was once me. She's manipulating you."

"Sheila, I'm well aware of Diana's antics and whatever she's planning isn't going to work. I'm just getting to know Zoe and I don't want to alienate her mother."

"You're afraid she's going to take your daughter away. Is that it?"

Sheila looked up at Nicholas, her heart twisting at the earnest, perplexed look in his gray eyes. He ran his hand across the waves in his close-cut hair. She followed the movement with her eyes, remembering his touch.

Two teenage boys with knits hats on their heads and puffer jackets jostled their way through the crowd, bumping Sheila's shoulder throwing off her fragile balance. She stumbled against Nicholas, and he caught her against him.

"Ma'am, I'm so sorry," one of them said. "Are you okay?"

"I'm fine," Sheila responded. "Thank you for asking."

"I didn't mean to run into you like that. I was playing around with my friend here."

"It's okay," she reassured him.

"They need to be more careful," Nicholas muttered. "Come on, let's find someplace to sit down."

Sheila didn't resist.

He led her into a little coffee shop that wasn't busy.

Nicholas settled her into a narrow booth and signaled the waitress for two cups of coffee. Sheila wasn't much of a coffee drinker these days, but she didn't protest.

The coffees arrived.

Nicholas added a packet of sweetener to his. Sheila stirred in cream.

Tears stung her eyes. This is what Sheila wanted to avoid —another confrontation with Diana.

"As much as I'd like to be there with you, I think it's best my children and I spend Christmas here at home," she said. "I know your family will be wonderful, but I'm tired of your ex-wife's antics. There are times I get the feeling that Zoe doesn't particularly like me either. Now that she has you in her life—I'm not sure she's willing to share you with Gray and Kiya."

"You know I wouldn't put you or them in an awkward position. I'll keep Diana in line, Sheila. I give you my word."

When she didn't respond, he asked, "Do you think it'll be that difficult to get along with Diana on Christmas Day?"

"I'm not willing to try, Nicholas." She paused a moment, then said, "I shouldn't have said that. It's just…"

He looked sad. "I thought it might be possible for us to be a family."

"Nicholas, do you really think Diana would ever make this possible? She wants you for herself."

"She had me and then she just walked out of our marriage. It's been over a long time for me." He looked down into his coffee. It was getting cold, but he waved the waitress off when she offered to refill their cups. "The only woman I want is you. I want to spend Christmas with you along with your children and Zoe."

"It really means this much to you?"

"Yes," Nicholas responded. "I won't invite Diana if she's a dealbreaker."

"Now that's not going to be easy," Sheila responded. "She'll try and make you feel guilty."

"She has family in Brunswick. If Diana insists on coming, she can stay with them."

"Babe, I'm telling you... that woman has no intentions of spending the holidays without you."

"I won't give her a choice," Nicholas responded.

They walked in silence with Sheila softly humming a Christmas carol.

Nicholas paused in his steps. "You've never been one for Christmas songs."

Sheila broke into a smile. "I've told you many times... I'm not the same person I used to be."

They left the mall and stopped to select a Christmas tree.

Kiya and Gray were waiting for them when they arrived. Gray helped Nicholas bring the tree inside the house.

"I love this time of year," Kiya said. She'd already retrieved the ornaments from the garage.

"Let's decorate this tree," Sheila said. "This is going to be the best Christmas ever."

Chapter 23

WHEN NICHOLAS ARRIVED HOME, he found Zoe at the house decorating the tree. Even though they had their own house, his daughter had a key to his place. He greeted her with a smile.

"I hope you don't mind I just showed up here. I was actually hoping to surprise you by having everything all decorated," she said.

Nicholas felt a shred of guilt for not including her when he went to Sheila's to decorate their tree. He would have to do better. He didn't want to risk alienating Zoe.

"Do I smell cookies?" he inquired, sniffing the air.

"You do. Mama's in the kitchen baking them. She makes the best gingerbread cookies."

"*Diana's here*?" Nicholas didn't mind Zoe coming over, but he preferred having advance knowledge whenever his ex-wife planned to join her.

"I sure am," a feminine voice said behind him. "You know how much I love Christmas." Carrying a plate of freshly baked gingerbread cookies, Diana walked over to him. "These used to be your favorites."

"I don't really eat sweets anymore," he responded. "I appreciate the gesture though."

Her smile disappeared. "I see."

Nicholas turned to face his daughter. "I'm glad you were able to find the decorations."

"I hope you don't mind, but I brought some of the ones I made growing up."

He smiled. "I don't mind at all, Zoe. I'm honored."

Diana began taking pictures of Nicholas and their daughter as they decorated the tree. He had a feeling they would end up on social media to attempt to make Sheila feel some type of way.

"Zoe tells me that you're going to Brunswick for Christmas," Diana said after the tree was decorated. They had settled in the living room, eating cookies and drinking hot chocolate.

"I am. I'd like for Zoe to meet the rest of her family." He bit into his cookie.

Diana wiped her mouth on her napkin. "What about me?" she asked. "I'd like to see everyone."

Nicholas met her gaze. "Why?"

"They were once my family, too," Diana stated. "Besides, my family lives in Brunswick as well."

"I figured you'd spend time with them."

"I assure you're planning to take Sheila and her kids down there."

"I invited them," Nicholas confirmed.

"I really feel this should be a family trip... for *us*."

"Although you refuse to acknowledge it, Sheila and her children are a part of my family. They are my future, Diana."

"What about me, Nick? Do you not feel *anything* for me? The mother of your only child."

"You walked out on our marriage, Diana. That was you. Not me."

"I've already apologized for my actions. I was wrong. I was only doing what I thought was right by you at the time."

"It no longer matters," Nicholas responded. "I can't stop you from going to Brunswick, but I'm telling you...it will be best that you plan to spend Christmas with your family. I want Sheila to feel comfortable."

"What about Zoe? Do you care about her comfort at all?"

"Of course, I do."

Lowering her voice, Diana said, "I didn't want to tell you this, but you need to know. Your daughter isn't fond of Sheila or her children. Zoe feels that you put them before her."

"Why hasn't she said anything to me about this?"

"You have to understand she and I talk about everything, Nick. She's just not that comfortable with you yet. You have to give her some time."

SHEILA WAS SITTING at the oak dining table, papers spread in a semicircle around her. She didn't look up for a moment. Her head was bent to her work; her locs, catching light from the crystal-and-stainless steel chandelier, brushed her cheek.

"Hey, mama," Gray said, setting his glass of milk and a plate of brownies down on the table. "Mind if I join you?"

"Of course not, sweetie." She looked up, smiled and gestured to a chair. "I don't mind at all."

Instead of sitting opposite her at the table, Gray moved to the chair next to her and pulled the brownies and the glass of milk toward him.

"What are you studying?"

"Jake sent over some stuff he wants me to look at. I worked with this company some years ago, so he wants my input," she said, making a face. "Every time I try to leave the business behind… they pull me back in."

"Well, you are still a partner," Gray stated between bites of his brownie.

"I do miss it sometimes."

"Then why don't you go back?"

"I have a different life now." Sheila eyed her son. "Have you been working on your essay for USC?"

Gray broke into a grin. "*Yes*, I have… Kiya's gonna read it and give me some feedback." He finished off his glass of milk, then asked, "Would you like to read it?"

"I would," Sheila responded. "I already know that it's great. You and Kiya both have a gift when it comes to writing."

"Mama, you think everything we do is great."

"And I'm your mother, so I know what I'm talking about."

Gray planted a wet kiss on her cheek, sparking laughter from her.

————————————

THE NEXT DAY, Sheila went shopping with Kiya for a gift for Nicholas. She'd seen him eyeballing a certain watch in the jewelry store the last time they were at the mall together.

Pointing it out to her daughter, she said, "This is the one."

"Oh, I like it."

"You think I should get the watch for him?"

Kiya nodded. "He's going to love it, Mama."

When the salesclerk walked over, Sheila asked, "I'd like to see this one please." She wanted to take a closer look at the Maurice Lacroix watch with stainless steel strap and sapphire dial. "It's really a stunning watch."

"And expensive."

Sheila smiled. "He's worth it."

After their purchase, she and Kiya decided to grab some lunch.

"What are you in the mood to eat?" Sheila asked. The hairs on her body stood up and caused her to stop in her tracks.

"What's wrong?"

Sheila's eyes traveled, searching her surroundings. "It's nothing," she said finally.

They decided to eat at the burger restaurant right outside the mall.

"What happened back there?" Kiya inquired.

"I just had a feeling that someone was watching us. The last time I felt it was when I first met Diana."

"She could be here at the mall," Kiya stated.

Picking up her menu, Sheila stated, "You're right. I just don't want to run into her. I'm enjoying my day and I want to keep enjoying it."

Chapter 24

DIANA SAT in a booth on the other side of Sheila and Kiya. They were separated by a thin wall. She could hear their entire conversation. She bristled at the mention of her name, but didn't alert them to her presence.

Sheila was grinning. "I saw him looking at it the last time we were here shopping. He even asked to try it on. It's perfect and he won't be expecting it."

She'd seen them at the precise moment they entered the jewelry store. Diana knew the watch they were talking about. Sheila was right—Nick was going to love it. She glanced over at the shopping bag with the exact same watch in it.

Diana planned to present her gift to him on Christmas Eve. She couldn't wait to see Sheila's face when she gave Nicholas the watch. He was going to be thrilled. She'd had to pawn her wedding rings just to pay for it, but like Sheila said earlier, Nicholas was worth it.

Just the idea made her giddy. She had to stifle her giggles by placing her hand over her mouth.

CHRISTMAS EVE HAD ARRIVED.

They got out of the SUV and walked up the steps and into Lily Belle and Pete Reynold's house. Kiya, Zoe, and Gray followed behind them, each one carrying a bag of groceries.

Nicholas greeted his aunt with a hug. "We stopped at the store when we came into town." he stated as he filled a bowl on the countertop with apples and oranges. He picked up a bunch of ripe, yellow bananas and piled them on top.

He tilted his head and watched Sheila, taking the remaining grocery items out the bag while his aunt put them away.

"I'm so glad you and the children decided to spend Christmas with us, Sheila."

"Thank you for having us, Mrs Reynolds."

"It's so good to see everyone again." Lily Belle picked up her keys and purse. "The kids and I are going out for a bit. Nicholas, can you take out the chicken I have in the refrigerator? That's for dinner tonight."

"Yes ma'am. Anything else you need me to do?"

"Entertain Sheila," she said with a wink. "We'll be back after a while."

Sheila chuckled. "She's something else… your aunt."

"She's always been a romantic. Plus, she knows how much I love you."

Nicholas sliced bread as he talked, gesturing broadly with the knife. He raised his voice, as though lecturing in a classroom.

Sheila gave a short laugh.

"What's so funny?"

"You sound like you're in teacher mode. I love it."

His eyes locked with hers. After what seemed like an eternity, he spoke. "I'm glad you decided to spend Christmas with me," Nicholas said before turning back to the sandwiches he was making. "Would you like some soup? It's homemade."

"Is it your aunt's vegetable soup?"

"Yeah."

"I definitely want some of that," Sheila said. "I need to get her recipe."

"Good luck with that. She won't even give it to me. Aunt Lily swears it's her fried chicken and vegetable soup that keeps me coming home."

"The kids seem to get along pretty well, don't you think?" Sheila asked. "Zoe and Kiya talked most of the drive here."

Nicholas gave a slight nod. "They seem to be forging a relationship on their own. I'm glad. I love the way they include Gray."

"Me too," she said.

When Lily Belle returned, the girls were talking up a storm about college. Every now and then, Gray would join the conversation.

Sheila released a short sigh of contentment. The holiday celebration was off to a great start.

No Diana—at least for the time being.

She made her way out on the patio. Sheila stood there looking up at the moon.

Nicholas walked up behind her, pulling her close to him. "I hope you're enjoying yourself."

"I am," Sheila confirmed. "I'm really having a great time."

He held her snugly. Her soft curves molded to the contours of his lean muscular body.

"You feel good," he whispered, his breath hot against her ear.

"So do you."

They pulled apart when they heard the girls coming toward them.

Nicholas escorted Sheila back into the house.

Ten minutes later, everyone was gathered around the table.

The doorbell rang.

"Now who can that be?" Pete asked, pushing away from the table.

Nicholas and Sheila exchanged glances. She knew instinctively the identity of this uninvited guest.

"Merry Christmas," Diana greeted. "Oh great... I made it just in time for dinner." She placed a hand on her daughter's shoulder. "Move down to the other end of the table."

Zoe looked horrified.

"Diana, you're the last one to the table, you come sit over here," Lily Belle stated.

Sheila couldn't believe the gall of Nicholas's ex-wife. She didn't have one ounce of shame in her.

So much for enjoying a drama-free evening...

IT WAS a tradition in Nicholas's family to open one gift on Christmas Eve.

After dinner, everyone gathered near the fireplace; on large floor pillows, chairs, wherever there was space.

"Nick, open mine first," Diana insisted.

"She's an eager beaver," Sheila muttered to herself. She hadn't realized she'd said it loud enough for Amara to overhear until she broke out in laughter.

"Sorry..."

"I completely agree," Amara whispered.

Nicholas opened the gift. His eyebrows rose in surprise upon seeing the watch. His gaze bore into Sheila in silent expectation. "Diana... this is a very nice gift, but it's too expensive."

"I saved up for it," She responded with a grin. "You've been so good to me and Zoe. This is just a small token of my appreciation in gratitude for all you've done for us."

Sheila noted Diana's wedding ring was missing on her finger. She held her composure, but deep down she was furious. She didn't know how Diana found out, but that watch wasn't just something random she decided to buy for Nicholas. This was intentional.

She could feel Diana's gaze on her but refused to look her way. She didn't want to give her the satisfaction of seeing her upset. The watch wasn't the only gift she'd purchased for

Nicholas. The one she planned to give him tonight was more personal and one she knew he'd appreciated. She was going to give him the watch on tomorrow, but Sheila had a host of others gifts she'd give him instead.

"Sheila, why don't you give him your present?" Diana suggested.

"I was thinking we'd let the kids give their gifts."

Kiya broke into a grin when she met her mother's gaze. "No, give him yours, mama."

Sheila handed a beautifully wrapped present to Nicholas.

He peered closely at the paper and smiled at her. "Quotes from my favorite author. I hate to rip it off."

Nicholas took his time opening the gift.

Sheila glanced up at Diana who seemed perplexed by what was happening.

Inside was a tee-shirt and a smaller box.

He looked up at Sheila. "Is this…"

She nodded.

"It's a tee-shirt with words on it," Diana mumbled. "They're so small you can't even read it."

"That's because his first book is printed on the shirt," Sheila explained. *The entire book.*"

"I love this…" Nicholas leaned over and kissed her. "Thank you, sweetheart. Wow… you really put a lot of thought into this."

"There's another inside," she told him.

Nicholas reached in and opened the smaller box. He burst into laughter. "Novel Teas…"

"You drink a lot of tea when you're writing, so I thought it would be nice to have some motivation while drinking. Each one features a quote from all of your favorite authors."

"This is great."

Sheila glanced over at Diana and grinned. Although she didn't say it aloud, she knew her message had been received.

I always have a backup plan.

Chapter 25

DIANA WAS fit to be tied. She couldn't believe how Nicholas had reacted over a tee-shirt with tiny words written all over it. You would've thought he'd won the lottery.

A *tee-shirt*.

Then the package of herbal teas with quotes…

I can't believe this insanity.

She'd spent a lot of money on a watch he barely looked at twice—the same exact watch Sheila purchased for him.

Diana started to feel as if she'd been played for a fool. Did they know she was following them at the mall? She'd been so careful, but maybe not careful enough.

This didn't turn out the way she'd expected but Diana wasn't ready to throw in her hand. She had one more card to play when the time was right.

SHEILA WATCHED as Diana prepared glasses of eggnog with brandy for the adults. She noticed that every once in a while she would glance over her shoulder to see if anyone was looking in her direction before pouring a tiny vial of powder in one glass.

She gave the one containing the drug to Nicholas.

When Diana strolled back into the kitchen, Sheila walked over, taking his glass and gave him hers.

Puzzled, he looked at her.

"Just trust me…"

Sheila debated whether to clue Nicholas in on what was about to transpire, but she decided to handle this herself. She was tired of Diana trying to manipulate her way into their lives. Sheila intended to put an end to this once and for all.

DIANA BIT BACK a smile as Nicholas downed his egg nog.

Not too long after, he yawned. "I don't know about y'all but I'm going to call it a night."

"You're not gonna wait up for Santa?" Diana asked.

"Nope. He doesn't exist."

Sheila rose up to her full height. "Good night everyone."

Diana helped clean up the kitchen before going to her room. Once she was sure everyone was asleep, she crept to the guest bathroom, changed into a sexy sheer teddy, then tiptoed toward Nicholas's room.

"You're wasting your time," Sheila said in a loud whisper,

startling Diana. "The best thing for you to do is leave now before you embarrass yourself and your daughter."

"You're afraid that Nick's gonna want me and not you. After all, I can offer him so much more."

"Actually, go for it," Sheila stated with a nonchalant shrug. "If you think he's going to give into this pathetic attempt at seduction. He didn't the first time and he won't this time either." She pointed to the closed bedroom door. "Go on…"

Diana glared at her.

"I saw you put something in his drink, so I switched his with mine."

"I don't know what you're talking about."

Sheila shook her head in dismay. "Whatever…"

Diana shivered.

"Maybe you should put your clothes back on and go to your parent's place. You might want to be quick about it. I hear Nicholas's mom moving around."

She rolled her eyes at Sheila before making her way back to the bathroom.

Diana dressed quickly, then walked out to find Sheila still in the hallway.

"I'll lock up behind you."

"You witch…" she uttered.

"Merry Christmas to you, too."

Nicholas's door opened just as Sheila eased past his room.

"What are you still doing up?" he asked.

"You were supposed to be sleeping," she said.

"I thought I heard voices out here."

Sheila shook her head no. "Just me." She decided not to tell him about Diana's antics because she didn't want to ruin the holidays for Zoe or for Nicholas.

Chapter 26

NICHOLAS WAS UP bright and early Christmas morning. While he was in the kitchen making breakfast, Sheila joined him.

He handed her a cup of herbal tea. "Merry Christmas, sweetheart."

"Merry Christmas, Nicholas."

"Are you going to tell me what really happened last night?"

"Let's just say that your ex was up to her old tricks."

"I figured as much."

Sheila made her way into the kitchen to help with the cooking. "I'll fry the bacon."

"Thanks sweetheart."

She glanced at him. "For what?"

"For everything."

By the time breakfast was ready, everyone in the house was up and moving about.

An hour later, they gathered in the living room to open up gifts.

Nicholas wasn't sure what he was going to say, but he knew that it was time for him to make a move.

He embraced Sheila, holding her tight.

Nicholas inhaled deeply, taking in the light floral scent of her body spray. "Family, I want y'all to know that I love this lady right here with my whole heart."

Sheila's eyes grew wet with unshed tears. "Babe, I love you too, but …"

He put a finger to her lips.

"When I walked away ten years ago, I realized something important—what we have is worth fighting for." Nicholas pulled out a tiny velvet box.

"Zoe and Kiya squealed in delight.

"Sheila Moore, will you do me the honor of being my wife?"

She was speechless. Fifty-two years old and this young, handsome man wanted to marry her. Sheila's eyes bounced around the room.

Lily Belle and Pete were smiling. Kiya had tears in her eyes, while Gray and Zoe stood there with grins on their faces.

Nicholas had chosen a diamond encrusted wedding band in platinum.

Sheila wiped away her tears. "You really know how to surprise a girl."

"You haven't answered my question," he responded. "Will you marry me? I'm thinking we should be able to plan a ceremony in a couple of months. I'm thinking we should make this official on Valentine's Day."

Sheila gasped in surprise. "You've already got this figured out."

Nicholas nodded. "I'd marry you tomorrow if I thought you'd agree to it."

She gazed into his eyes and saw the love reflected there. "You really want this?"

"More than anything else in the world," he responded with a grin. "I can't see my life without you in it. Now will you please answer the question?"

"Of course, I'll marry you, Nicholas."

Sheila glanced down at the ring he was about to place on her finger. "I would be honored to marry you on February 14th."

Kiya squealed and began jumping up and down.

Amara entered the room carrying a bottle of Champagne. "I hear we're having a wedding soon. Congratulations." Her husband followed with a bottle of sparkling cider for the teens.

Sheila hugged Nicholas. "Yes, we are."

Sheila was giddy with happiness for the rest of the day. Not even Diana's appearance could dim her mood. She had no doubts about Nicholas and was finally free to love him with her whole heart.

The moment Diana spied the ring on her left hand, she said, "Is that what I think it is?"

"They're getting married," Zoe announced.

"I see."

She looked as if she were about to break down into tears, but she managed to hold her composure. After a moment, she stood up. "I'm having dinner with my family, so I'd better get going. I came to bring over the presents."

"Aren't you gonna congratulate the happy couple?" Lily Belle asked.

"Actually, I'm not because I'm not in agreement with this. She's not right for him."

"Says the woman who abandoned her husband for another man," Lily Belle commented. "The fact of the matter is they don't need your blessing or your congratulations, dear. I just wanted to give you the opportunity to show you were raised right."

Diana sent a sharp glare in Lily Belle's direction. "That marriage is never gonna happen." She stormed out of the house without waiting for a response.

"Well, that was rude…" Gray stated.

"I'm so sorry," Zoe said. "She's just upset by the news."

Sheila smiled. "It's fine, sweetie."

Later that evening, Nicholas and Sheila settled in the living room while everyone else was in another room watching Christmas movies.

"You've made me a very happy man," he told Sheila. "This time is forever."

She agreed. "My heart is clear. I'm certain that I want to spend the rest of my life with you and our children."

NICHOLAS AND SHEILA were on their first date of the new year.

His perfect teeth flashed white as he grinned. "I love that we're great together. We always seem to be on the same wavelength, totally in tune. Our interests, our goals, our values, they all click."

"That's what really counts, right?" Sheila asked. "These are the things that make for a strong friendship."

She pushed her half-eaten enchiladas aside to reach across the table and take Nicholas's hand. "So, where are we going to live?"

"I was thinking I'd sell my townhouse and buy a house big enough for all our children. I'd like to stay near the university."

"We need a five-bedroom house with an office for each of us and a pool."

They continued to discuss their plans for the future while they finished eating their lunch.

"If you'd like, I'll call my realtor and have her pull some listings for us unless you'd rather build a custom home."

"It's something we can definitely talk about," Nicholas responded. "Tonight, we can list the pros and cons of both."

Sheila smiled. "I like that idea."

"There's something I need to ask," he said.

"What is it?"

"Are you okay with me inviting Jake and Tori to the wedding?'

"Sure," Sheila responded. "It doesn't bother me to have them there. Charlene—that's another story. That girl hates me with a passion."

His gaze met hers. "I can't wait to marry you."

"We only have five weeks left before our big day."

"When you look at me like this—it feels like five years." Nicholas lowered his voice. "I can't wait to be with you."

Sheila fanned herself with her hand. "Okay, it's time to change the subject."

"WHAT ARE YOU DOING HERE?" Sheila asked when she found Diana standing on her porch.

Brushing past her, she stated, "I came to see you *obviously*."

Arms folded across her chest, Sheila demanded, "To discuss what? Because there's nothing to talk about where Nicholas is concerned."

"You think now that you're engaged to Nick that you've won?" Diana gave a short laugh. "Girl, this is far from over."

"Go on… get it out of your system. There's nothing you can do to change the outcome, but you're welcome to have your say, Diana."

"What can you truly offer Nick? You're much older than him; you need a cane to walk… you can't give him a child—I've already given him that."

"So, you keep saying," Sheila responded. "It's too bad that you weren't so proud of that fact years ago. How is it that you didn't think to verify your daughter's father back then? And is that the only child you kept from Nicholas?"

"Excuse me? What are you talking about?"

"I know about the abortion you had right before you married Nicholas," Sheila uttered.

Diana's mouth dropped open in her shock. When she found her voice, she said, "How dare you go looking into my personal business."

"Isn't that what you did to me by going to see Tori?" Shrugging in nonchalance, Sheila stated, "I thought that's what we were doing."

"That baby wasn't Nicholas, and you wonder why there's a huge question mark where Zoe is concerned. You came here with one purpose in mind, and it wasn't reuniting your daughter with my fiancé. I don't know what happened between you and your husband, but what I do know... this is all some huge ploy to get back in Nicholas's life. You just didn't count on him being involved with another woman. Your biggest mistake is that you didn't count on that woman being *me*."

"What's that supposed to mean?"

"I'm so much better at being manipulative—at least I used to be. Diana, give it up. Nicholas wants to marry me because he loves me. I didn't have to play any games to get him. In fact, I gave him up. I thought he deserved so much better than me."

"You made him feel sorry for you. Nick's always had a thing for stray animals."

Sheila laughed. "Perhaps, but I don't need him for anything, Diana. I have the Lord, money and my children... my life is good. If Nicholas changed his mind today about marrying me—it would hurt but I'll survive. Can you say the same?"

"If life is so good for you, then walk away, Sheila. I was Nick's first love and I hurt him terribly. Give me the chance to make it right."

"That's not my call, Diana. And to be perfectly honest, I'm not that *nice*."

"Zoe deserves her father's full attention. She shouldn't have to share him with children that aren't biologically his."

"It's your fault that she didn't have Nicholas in her life," Sheila stated. "You kept her away because either you really didn't know who fathered her or you thought you'd have a better life with Steve." She met Diana's gaze. "I can look in her eyes and see that I'm right."

"You don't know a thing about me."

"Oh, I know a whole lot more than you think…"

"You're bluffing. If you knew anything—you'd go running straight to Nick with the information."

"Actually, I wouldn't. I'm not like you, Diana. I don't want to cause Nicholas more pain—I'd rather spare him."

"Oh, you're so frigging noble."

"No, I'm not," Sheila countered. "I've just learned there are consequences for every action good or bad. Diana, get this straight in your brain… Nicholas and I are going to get married. He is adopting my children—there is nothing you can do to stop anything. I suggest you go home to work on your marriage or dissolve it—it doesn't matter which to me. Just stay out of our lives."

"I will be around as long as Zoe is here. She is Nick's child and that makes me a part of *his* family."

"I don't care about that, Diana. Not as long as you respect boundaries."

"Did Nick tell you that he had me in his bed?"

Sheila didn't flinch. "He didn't have to tell me you tried to seduce him. I knew you would. I also know you made your move right after my mother died. I didn't want to believe you could be so heartless. Your actions told me a lot about your character."

"So, you believe that nothing happened between the two of us."

"*I know it.* Nicholas would've told me otherwise."

"I can't believe you're one of *those* women—the ones who believe everything a man says. You take it as the gospel truth."

"Diana, I know Nicholas. He's honest and loyal. I'm not going to let you plant doubts in my head about him."

"Mom, why are you here?" Zoe asked.

"The question is what are you doing here?"

"Kiya and I had lunch and did some shopping."

"So now you're sneaking behind my back?"

"I wouldn't have to if you'd stop the drama," Zoe responded. "Sheila isn't the blame for anything, Mom. Everyone is trying to get along except *you*."

"You forget yourself, young lady."

"Please go home."

"You two go upstairs," Sheila stated. "Diana and I are talking. There's nothing to worry about. *Really*."

The girls went to Kiya's room.

Diana glanced over her shoulder, then back at Sheila. "Why didn't you tell me Zoe was here?"

"You never gave me a chance to do so," she responded.

"You wanted her to hear us," Diana accused. "You're trying to turn my daughter against me."

"I'm not trying to do anything like that."

"Don't you dare try to turn Nick against me, Sheila. I know you're gonna run straight to him to tell him about our discussion."

"That particular thought hadn't crossed my mind. I have no intention of spoiling my evening with Nicholas by mentioning you."

Diana glared at her.

"Goodbye Diana," Sheila stated. "It's time for you to leave my house. Do me a favor and don't come back here unless you're invited."

Chapter 27

WHEN NICHOLAS ARRIVED, he seemed a bit subdued.

"Are you okay?" Sheila asked.

He handed her a letter. "This came today. It's from Diana's husband."

Nicholas,

There are some things you need to know about your former wife. Understand that I love her, but I know who I married. She has never been faithful to you. She was forced to have an abortion before your wedding because she didn't know if you were the father. She left you when she discovered she was pregnant again, but this time I was told that the child was mine. She had me believing that the two of you no longer shared a bed.

I admit I have been just as much a fool as you, but I still love Diana and I want our marriage. We still have two young boys who yearn daily for their mother. Her sudden interest in you is your fame and fortune. I'm pretty sure she's told you that Zoe is your daughter and not mine. It is true that I am not her biological father, but I've loved her as my own and that will never change.

I would advise you to have a DNA test done as I was not the only man she was cheating on you with—this is not a letter written to hurt my wife—only a plea for help to persuade her to come back home where she belongs.

Best Regards,

Steve

Sheila was speechless.

"She may not be my daughter," Nicholas said in a low voice.

"Babe…"

"Is it true?" Zoe interjected.

"I didn't know you were here." Nicholas glanced over at Sheila who said, "I was just about to tell you."

Zoe's eyes filled with tears.

Nicholas embraced her. "Please don't cry. I know in my heart that you're *my* daughter."

"But I want to know for sure."

"We can do that," Nicholas said. "But I don't need a DNA test to tell me what I already know to be true."

Sheila's heart broke for them both.

"WHERE HAVE YOU BEEN?" Diana asked when Zoe entered the house the next day. "I kept calling you and all I got was a text saying you were staying with Nick. I expected you home an hour ago."

"We took a DNA test. I didn't realize it would take as long as it did."

"You did *what*?"

"Nicholas and I had a DNA test done. We want to know if what you've been telling us is the truth."

"I can't believe he did this to you." Diana was furious with Nicholas. "I'm going over there right now to have it out with him."

"Mom, it was my idea," Zoe interjected.

"Why? I *told* you he was your father. I don't have a reason to lie."

"Then what's the big deal? Why are you acting like this?"

"Because it makes me look as if I was just out in the streets with other men. Like I don't know who fathered my child. I made one mistake. *One*."

"This isn't about you," Zoe responded. "This is about me. Nicholas Washington is a good man, and he shouldn't be lied to or manipulated. I've already lost one father... I don't want to go through that a second time."

"Nick's the one dictating all the shots around here," Diana stated bitterly. "He hasn't offered one penny of back child support to me, but now he's trying to manipulate you into thinking I'm the with the hidden agenda."

"Are you for real right now?" Zoe asked. "Mom, I've lived with you my whole life. I know what you do when you don't get your way. You came to Nicholas because Steve didn't get his father's inheritance. That's when suddenly you start questioning if he was really my dad."

"You've been listening to Nick and Sheila. They're the ones filling your head with this nonsense."

"You're not paying for this house we're living in, Mom because of me. If it turns out that Nicholas is my dad, I can attend college where he teaches for free. I also know that he does give you a monthly allowance as well."

"That man has made millions, Zoe. You should have a trust fund. *You* are his only child. I bet he's already set up trusts for Sheila's children."

"So what? I'm not here for his money."

"I was the one who worked two jobs so he could pursue his passion," Diana uttered. "He owes me."

Zoe eyed her in complete disbelief. "This has always been your plan. You didn't bring me here to meet my dad. You came here hoping to get money."

"Your father wouldn't be the success he is if it hadn't been for my sacrifices."

Diana grabbed her purse. "I'll be back. I need to get some things off my chest."

She walked briskly out the house and got into her car.

Ten minutes later, she pulled into Nicholas's driveway. He met her outside .

"Zoe and I had a DNA test done earlier."

"She told me," Diana stated. "I really don't appreciate you going behind my back like this."

"Zoe actually suggested we do it while we were having breakfast."

"Because she wanted to please you. That's why, Nick. You could've refused her. All you had to do was reassure her that she is your daughter."

"Why does this upset you so much?" Nicholas asked. "Are you worried but anything?"

His question threw her for a moment. "What are you suggesting?"

"I get the feeling that you're still keeping secrets from me. Because if you are—now is the time to come clean."

"I'm n-not," Diana sputtered. "Where is this coming from? Did Sheila plant something in your head about me?"

"Sheila has nothing to do with this. This is strictly between you and me," Nicholas said. "Looking at the expression on your face right now... it's got guilty written all over it. You should've learned a long time ago that the truth has a way of coming to light."

"I have no idea what you're talking about."

"What about the baby you got rid of before we got married?" Nicholas asked. "I remember asking you if you were pregnant and you told me no."

"I wasn't."

"Diana, you're lying."

She released a long sigh, then said, "Nick, I had a miscarriage back then. There was no point in talking about it. I was hurt and just wanted to focus on our wedding. You were so happy—I didn't want to make you sad."

"A miscarriage, huh..."

"Yeah. I lost the baby," Diana said. "I had to have a procedure after called a D & C. There wasn't an abortion."

"I'm assuming you have medical records to back this up."

"I do, but I'm not about to let you see them. Nick, I don't have to lie to you about this."

"But you have… many times," he responded. "So, forgive me if I don't take your word as the gospel." Nicholas paused a moment before saying, "Were you carrying my child? The baby you lost. I want to know the truth."

"I can't believe you'd ask me this."

"Answer the question, Diana and before you do—I already know the truth."

"The truth is I don't know if it was your child or not." Tears filled her eyes. "That's what you wanted to hear. It's what you think anyway."

Nicholas wasn't moved by her tears. "Go home Diana. I don't want to see or hear from you until after the results of the DNA test come back."

SHEILA STOOD in front of three full-length mirrors in the bridal boutique eyeing the gown from different angles.

"I like this one," Kiya said as she fingered the soft draping at the bottom of the ivory-colored wedding dress.

"It's beautiful," Sheila agreed. The silky satin was well-suited to a winter wedding, without weighing down the dress. The pearl embroidered scoop neck and full-length sleeves, gathered at the shoulder, worked beautifully on Sheila's slender frame. She'd decided against a train. She chose a pearl encrusted headband which matched the edging of the bodice on the gown.

"This dress looks so beautiful on you."

Sheila nodded in agreement. "I actually like it better than the one I saw at the other store. It was nice but not exactly what I had in mind. This dress is perfect."

"A few nips and tucks and you'll be good to go," the owner of the boutique said. "The dress needs very little adjustments."

Sheila turned away from the mirror with a smile.

"Have you decided on a color for the bridesmaid dresses?"

"There are only two bridesmaids: my daughter and soon-to-be stepdaughter," she responded.

Sheila removed the gown with Kiya's assistance.

"Have you talked to Zoe?' she asked while getting dressed.

"She's okay. Angry and disappointed in her mother right now though."

"I pray those tests confirm that Nicholas is her father," Sheila said.

"Me too," Kiya responded. "They deserve a happy ending."

Chapter 28

DIANA OPENED the door to find Nicholas with Sheila standing on the porch. Her eyes strayed to the white envelope in his hand. She stepped aside to let them enter.

Zoe met them in the living room. "Are those the DNA results?"

"Is there something you want to tell me before I read the results?" he asked his ex-wife.

Diana chewed on her bottom lip. "What is *she* here for?"

"I'm here for the truth," Sheila responded. "We all want to get this part over and done with."

Diana sent her a sharp glare. "You're not married to Nick yet. This has nothing to do with you."

"I asked Sheila to come with me," Nicholas interjected. "I've been trying to figure out why you seem so worried about this DNA test."

"I told him it was because you're leaving out something,"

Sheila interjected. "If you were a hundred percent sure that Nicholas is Zoe's father—this wouldn't have been an issue at all."

Zoe glanced at her mother. "Mom... we all deserve the truth."

"I know all about you Sheila Moore," Diana uttered. "I know how you tried to break up Jake and Tori's marriage. You're nothing but a home wrecker."

"I know a little something about you as well. Steve left his wife and married you because you told him that you were carrying his child. He wrote a letter to Nicholas and told him everything. Despite all the lies you told him—he still loves you and wants to make his marriage work. It's obvious that we've both made mistakes in the past. I own my mess. It's time for you to do the same."

Zoe eyed her mother, then pointed to the envelope in Nicholas's hand. "Is there a possibility that he is not my father?"

Diana met her daughter's gaze. "Sweetheart..."

"No, I want to know the truth. I spoke to Daddy... I mean Steve... Mom. He told me that he didn't put us out like you claimed. He told me that you've been obsessed with Nicholas for years. He said that you came to him and told him that he was not my father. He never had any suspicions otherwise."

"Zoe, he's lying to you."

"He's not the one lying, Mama. He sent me a copy of the DNA test *you* ordered. Steve said you were looking for a way to re-insert yourself back in Nicholas's life. He also said you were involved with another man when he met you."

Diana didn't respond.

"Is Nicholas my father or is there someone else?"

After a short pause, Diana said, "I don't know. There is another possibility, but he's deceased."

Zoe burst into tears.

Diana glared at Nicholas and Sheila. "I hope you're happy now. This is all your fault." When she reached for her daughter, Zoe retreated a step back.

"No, this is all your doing," Zoe shot back.

Looking at Nicholas, Diana said, "Let's just get this over with. I can't stand to be around *her* anymore. I'm just done."

Nicholas opened the envelope and pulled out the contents. He gazed at Zoe and said, "This confirms what I've known in my heart from the first day I met you. You're *my* daughter."

Diana released an audible sigh of relief while Zoe burst into a second bout of crying. She rushed into her father's arms. "I'm so glad you're my dad because I love you."

"I love you, too," Nicholas responded.

Tears filled Diana's eyes. "Zoe…"

"I can't talk to you right now, Mom. I'm going for a walk."

When Zoe left the house, Nicholas turned to his ex-wife. "I hope we can now move forward and leave the stupid stuff behind us. Sheila and I are going to be married. I'm going to adopt her children and I'm telling you now—don't try to mess with my family."

"Does Zoe know your plans?" Diana asked.

"She was the first person I discussed it with and she's thrilled to have Kiya and Gray as siblings."

"I know my daughter. She has no choice but to be okay with this—it's not like she could change your mind."

"Diana, you really need to quit," Sheila uttered. "I've stood back and let Nicholas deal with you, but I've had enough of your nonsense. You left this man years ago; you didn't tell him about the pregnancy, and you married another man. Now you suddenly think you have the right to prance back into his life like nothing happened. You're doing the same thing to Steve that you did to Nicholas."

"I've told you before... don't try to act like you're better than me, Sheila."

"That's not it at all," she responded. "I'm trying to help you. You have a chance to do things differently from this point forward. You have two sons to think about. I'm sure they're missing their mother."

A tear rolled down Diana's cheek.

"Nicholas and I are going to be married soon. I'll never try to take your place in Zoe's life. I'm happy just being part of her support system. I don't have an issue with you unless you try to bring drama in our lives. I'm not looking to be your friend—frankly, I'm not even interested in that. However, we will have to be around each other. Let's just try to be peaceful toward one another."

"I need to make sure my daughter's okay." Diana gestured toward the door. "I'd like y'all to leave." She was not going to let Sheila know that she'd gotten under her skin.

Zoe returned home an hour later.

"I was getting worried about you," Diana said. "You didn't answer your phone when I called."

"I didn't feel like talking."

"And now?"

"How could you treat Steve like this?" Zoe asked. "He's been good to us. Why would you lie and use me to leave him?"

"I was looking out for you."

"Mom, you were looking out for yourself. Be honest..."

"I'm sorry, Zoe. I didn't handle this the right way. But in my defense, I truly didn't believe you were Nick's child when I was pregnant. I never would've left him if I'd known the truth. I panicked." Diana shook her head sadly. "He's never going to forgive me."

"He's already forgiven you, Mom," Zoe stated. "He will never take you back and you have to accept that. He's in love with Sheila. They're good together."

"What is he going to do if her MS worsens?"

"He will take care of her. So, will the rest of us."

Diana stared at Zoe. "You'd be Sheila's caregiver?"

"Yeah, I'd help out. Mom, she's been really nice to me."

"Just wait until she becomes Mrs. Washington... you'll see the real Sheila after that. I promise you."

"Just leave her alone... please..."

"What about me, Zoe? Do you even care that my heart is broken? Nick promised that his heart would always belong to me."

Zoe sighed in resignation. "Mama, you left him years ago. How can you really expect Nicholas to trust you again? Why would he just give up what he has with Sheila for you—the woman who's done nothing but lie to him?"

Rubbing her temple, Diana mumbled, "I have a headache. I'm going to lie down for a bit."

As soon as Diana entered her bedroom, she collapsed on the bed in sobs. She'd lost Nicholas forever. What hurt most was that she lost him eighteen years ago when she chose money over love.

"I'M NOT HERE to cause trouble," Diana said when Nicholas arrived home two days later. "I came to tell you that I'm leaving town. I spoke with Steve and we're gonna try to see if our marriage can be repaired. *For the boys.*"

"I pray it works out for you."

"I'm sure you do."

"Diana, I wasn't the one who destroyed our marriage."

"I made a mistake, Nick. All I wanted was a second chance. You had no problem giving Sheila one after everything she did."

"Don't bring her into this. There will never be a you and me even if Sheila wasn't in the picture."

"You told me on our wedding night that you'd never love another woman. It's obvious that you lied to me."

"Oh, I lied..." He broke into a harsh laugh. "Did you think I'd sit and wait for you to show up one day like nothing happened?"

"Tori took Jake back after he cheated with Sheila."

"I'm not Tori and our situation is not the same, Diana. If you hadn't stepped out on our marriage—maybe, we would still be together... I don't know. Regardless, it's too late. I wish you well with Steve. It sounds like he's willing to give you a second chance. If I were you, I wouldn't blow this opportunity."

"You can be so cold, Nick."

"There's no point in rehashing this, Diana."

Her eyes filled with tears.

"Don't..." Nicholas uttered.

"I still love you."

"I'm sorry but I don't feel the same way."

Diana released a short sigh. "Are you okay with Zoe living here with you?"

"Of course, I am," he responded. "She and Kiya want to get an apartment together. I think they've already looked at a couple of places."

"Sounds great."

"You don't have to worry about Zoe. She's going to be fine."

Diana gave a slight nod. "I know you'll look after her. I'm not worried about that." She glanced down at her watch. "I need to get back to the house to finish packing. My flight leaves tonight."

"Safe travels," Nicholas said.

"I wish you were just a tiny bit sad over my leaving. It would show that you cared just a little bit. We were in love at one time."

"You need to stop trying to live in the past, Diana. That was a long time ago and I've moved on. You have a husband and I really hope you and Steve are able to work things out."

"We going to try," Diana responded. "I really don't have much of a choice."

"Zoe said he was a good man. And he's very much in love with you."

"He is," she confirmed. "I just don't feel the same."

"Not that you asked me for advice, but I'm going to offer some anyway… be honest with Steve. That's the only way to save your marriage. Once all the cards are on the table—you have the groundwork laid to either build or tear down your relationship. You have someone who loves you and he wants you to come home. He's willing to give you a second chance after everything you've done. That's real love, Diana."

"Why couldn't you have given me another chance?"

"Because our season ended almost nineteen years ago and I refuse to look backward. You should do the same. Look ahead and see what the future holds."

"Where have you been?" Zoe asked. "I thought we were going to have lunch together."

Diana sat down on the sofa. "I went to see Nick. I wanted him to know that I'm leaving. I wanted to say goodbye."

"Are you sure about this, Mom?"

Her gaze grew wet with unshed tears. "I can't stay here and watch him marry Sheila," Diana said. "I don't get it. She doesn't deserve a man like Nick. Look at all the horrible stuff she's done to Jake and Tori."

"To be honest, I don't see where you have much room to

talk," Zoe said. "Look at the stuff you did to try to break them up. It wasn't right either."

Diana sent a sharp glare in her daughter's direction. "You need to remember your place, Zoe."

"Mom, you're standing here judging a woman you haven't taken time to get to know. She's nothing like the person you described. She's a devoted mother and she really loves my dad. Besides, Jake and Tori forgave her."

Diana shook her head sadly. "After all the stuff I did for you—I never thought you'd turn on me."

"I haven't turned on you, but I'm also not going to take part in a scheme to manipulate my dad," Zoe said. "I love you but you're wrong and I'm not going to pretend otherwise. You lied to me and both my fathers. You weren't here to reunite me and Nicholas—you wanted money."

Diana was silent for a moment. She just sat there staring into space. After a moment, she responded, "I guess I should be on my way then. There's no place for me here in Charleston."

"Mom, I love you and I'm gonna miss you."

Touching Zoe's cheek, she said, "I'll miss you, too. You be careful and make sure you call me at least once a week."

"Don't act like I don't call you every day when we're apart. I'll be calling and texting you a lot. You're my mother and nothing will ever change that."

They embraced.

"My flight leaves tonight at seven," Diana announced. "We'll have a nice long lunch, then you can drop me off at the airport."

Chapter 29

THERE WAS a slight chill in the air, but the February weather was picture perfect for the Valentine's Day wedding ceremony.

In front of the ballroom, an arch decorated with flowing drapes of silk and organza in vibrant colors of red, pink and ivory. Floral arrangements of white roses adorned the altar. Three classical musicians played romantic selections as they waited for the ceremony to start.

Kiya and Zoe wore matching lace bridesmaid gowns with red taffeta sashes. Gray wore a black tux with red tie and vest while Nicholas chose to wear an ivory tux with a red bow tie and matching cummerbund.

In the dressing room, Amara secured a headband made of pearls and rhinestones on top of Sheila's head.

Kiya checked her watch. "It's almost time for the ceremony to begin."

She and Zoe left the room.

Gray knocked, then walked inside. "Are you ready to get married?" he asked.

"I never thought this day would come," she told him. "Nicholas and I getting married…"

He kissed her cheek. "Mama, you look beautiful."

"She sure does," Amara said, picking up Sheila's bouquet of red roses.

"Ready?" Gray asked.

"Son, I've been ready for this day a long time."

NICHOLAS SPOKE HIS VOWS FIRST. "Sheila, I take you to be my wife. I want you to know that I'll always cherish you. I won't ever take you for granted. I will always trust and respect you, be faithful and love you until the end of my life. Even then I'll love you for all eternity. I give you my heart, and my love, from this day forward for as long as we both shall live."

Sheila smiled through her tears. "Nicholas, I love you. You are my best friend, and after today, you'll be my lover and the father of my children. We have waited ten long years to get to this moment, and I want you to know that you were so worth the wait. I promise to love and cherish you through whatever life may bring us. I make this vow to you today and all the days of our life."

Neither Sheila nor Nicholas could contain their excitement when they heard the words that would make their union real.

"I now pronounce you man and wife…"

Nicholas exhaled a long sigh of pleasure. He pulled Sheila into his arms, drawing her close. He pressed his lips to hers for a meaningful kiss.

His eyes traveled down the length of her, nodding in obvious approval. "You look so beautiful, sweetheart. I love you, Mrs. Washington."

"I love you, too, Mr. Washington."

Sheila held up her hand to admire her wedding ring. "We did it, Nicholas. We're finally married."

He kissed her cheek. "Yes, we are."

The photographer that Nicholas hired took pictures of them alone and with family.

Afterward, they headed to a nearby estate they'd rented for a poolside reception. The patio had been transformed into a tropical paradise for the evening.

Tall, clear vases filled with water and a variety of fruits, and topped with pink, red and white roses made visually stunning centerpieces. Floating candles in the pool illuminated the water. Glass tables were arranged around the pool for guests to sit.

The musicians took their place near the fireplace and prepared to treat the guests with more soft, romantic music designed to accentuate the calming feel of the pool area and the beauty of the evening.

She couldn't be happier. Her wedding day was absolute perfection.

SHEILA CONTINUED to attend a monthly support group for MS. She'd been with this group for ten years and the attendees had become like family. Most of them were guests at her wedding to Nicholas six months ago.

"I'm having to use a walker more these past two weeks," she said. "As all of you know, this disease is so unpredictable. I'm not going to worry about what's happening to my body —I pay attention, but I don't worry. Instead, I work around my issue and live my life as normal as possible." Sheila paused when her eyes landed on Nicholas, who sat in the back of the room.

He winked at her.

"I'm thankful for each day the Lord gives me with my family. The one thing I want to leave with each of you tonight is this. We can't move forward looking in the rearview mirror. We mess up, but each day that we open our eyes—we get to write a new chapter. Nothing can change that. Not even multiple sclerosis. I still have good days and bad days, but regardless, I'm glad to be above ground."

The room exploded in applause. "MS isn't our friend, but it also doesn't have to be our enemy either."

At the end of the meeting, Nicholas escorted his wife to the car.

"I remember the first time you showed up at this meeting. It was after we broke up."

"I wanted to surprise you."

She smiled. "That you did. I remember you asking me if I'd changed my mind about becoming a mother. At that time,

I didn't think it was possible. Kiya and Gray are proof that all things are possible through the Lord."

"I told you back then that you'd make a great mother. I was right."

Sheila embraced him. "I could've kicked myself for letting you go back then."

Looking into his eyes, she murmured, "Thank you so much for opening up my heart and showing me that I was lovable. Thank you for coming back for me."

"Thank you for waiting on me."

"We have everything we want, love, marriage and a family. This is everything I've ever wanted in life. As far as I'm concerned—it can't get any better than this."

Nicholas kissed her. "I feel the same way. To be able to love and be loved—it's worth more than money. I hope that Diana will learn this fundamental truth one day."

"Let's go home to our kids. I'm sure they haven't bothered to pull anything out of the freezer for dinner. They're probably there waiting on us to cook."

He laughed. "I actually made dinner tonight. Kiya and Zoe are back on campus and Gray is supposed to be studying. I was thinking we'd have a late meal together before heading to the house."

"I love date nights…" Sheila said with a grin.

The Prodigal Series

The Prodigal Husband

Defining Moments

Unexpected Serenity

9 798743 182824